MW00640121

WITHDRAWN

Killa Kounty 3

Khufu

WITHDRAWN

JUL 2 0 202

Lock Down Publications and Ca$h
Presents

Killa Kounty 3

A Novel by *Khufu*

258780528

Khufu

Lock Down Publications
P.O. Box 944
Stockbridge, Ga 30281

Visit our website @
www.lockdownpublications.com

Copyright 2022 by Khufu
Killa Kounty 3

All rights reserved. No part of this book may be reproduced in any form or by electronic or mechanical means, including information storage and retrieval systems without permission in writing from the publisher, except by a reviewer who may quote brief passages in review.
First Edition October 2022
Printed in the United States of America

This is a work of fiction. Names, characters, places, and incidents either are products of the author's imagination or are used fictitiously. Any similarity to actual events or locales or persons, living or dead, is entirely coincidental.

Lock Down Publications
Like our page on Facebook: Lock Down Publications @
www.facebook.com/lockdownpublications.ldp

Book interior design by: **Shawn Walker**
Edited by: **Jill Alicea**

4

Stay Connected with Us!

Text **LOCKDOWN** to 22828 to stay up-to-date with new releases, sneak peaks, contests and more...
Thank you.

Submission Guideline.

Submit the first three chapters of your completed manuscript to ldpsubmissions@gmail.com, subject line: Your book's title. The manuscript must be in a .doc file and sent as an attachment. Document should be in Times New Roman, double spaced and in size 12 font. Also, provide your synopsis and full contact information. If sending multiple submissions, they must each be in a separate email.

Have a story but no way to send it electronically? You can still submit to LDP/Ca$h Presents. Send in the first three chapters, written or typed, of your completed manuscript to:

LDP: Submissions Dept
P.O. Box 944
Stockbridge, Ga 30281

DO NOT send original manuscript. Must be a duplicate.

Provide your synopsis and a cover letter containing your full contact information.

Thanks for considering LDP and Ca$h Presents.

Acknowledgments

To the creator for allowing its life force to run through me and experience this thing we call life. I wanna take a moment to salute Ca$h for taking a chance on me. The stepping stone you've provided me with is deeply appreciated and forever holds my regards. Thank you, big homie! To my loyal fans, I love y'all past forever. Without y'all, I am nothing. To the owner of *The Street Elements* magazine, Kevin…placing me in your issues means everythang to me. You a real one! To my ride or die queen…I love you for lovin' me the way you do despite my current situation. You a real Queen! To my mother…I love you, lady! You are my queen! Fort Pierce, Florida…stand up! Lockdown Publications over everything!

Dedications

I dedicate this book to everybody that stood in that courtroom with their heads high and remained forever solid! Free Quinton Bradley…Killa…C-Rock…Jeremy…Jihad…Jimmy Reeves. Rest In Power Lanetta…Stacey…Tela…Tayda.

~The only way to mourn a fallen soldier is to pick up the fallen weapon.~

Khufu

CHAPTER 1
CONTRACT KILLIN'

Khafre's phone ringing woke Samantha from a shallow sleep. She tapped Khafre on his chest in an attempt to wake him up, but to no avail.

"Khafre, baby, your phone is ringing!" exclaimed Samantha mildly. Khafre didn't move a muscle. Samantha pulled Khafre's dick out and sucked the head of it slowly. The warmth from her mouth caused Khafre to moan and squirm. Once Khafre grew in size, Samantha swallowed him whole and began to suck more aggressively. By this time, Khafre's phone had stopped ringing. Samantha's slurping awoke Hanna, who immediately joined in.

"Um, shit," moaned Khafre, now semi-conscious. Hanna and Samantha put Khafre's dick in their mouths in tandem until he came on both of their faces.

"Damn! You...nasty...bitches!" growled Khafre through clenched teeth.

The words "nasty bitches" must have been a trigger to some type of freak bitch trance, because as soon as those words left Khafre's mouth, Hanna and Samantha devoured each other. The moment they started eating each other out, Khafre's phone rang again.

"Yeah, what up?" answered Khafre, eyes glued on the sisters.

"Da fuck is that noise?" questioned Hezron.

"Deez bitches in here going wild!"

"You still wit' them hoes? Nigga, climb out da pussy for a minute! Pops wanna holla at'chu."

"'Bout what?" asked Khafre, his curiosity piqued.

"I'on know, he ain't say. Me and Machi finna head to Game Stop."

"A'ight, drop the addy."

"We in the same spot, fam. Tighten up," said Hezron.

"Aye!" Khafre hung up, and saw that the twins were still at it. "Aye! Y'all cut that shit out. We finna move out."

Khufu

***

Hanna and Samantha refused to go back to Naples, so Khafre got them a room on US-1 at the Red Roof Inn. A change of location was due to Khafre's paranoia. After the gravesite incident. Khafre refused to sleep in the same place twice. He left the twins in the hotel, and was now pulling into Offtop's luxurious home. Offtop had heavy surveillance, so he saw Khafre pulling up and met him at the door.

"What up, nephew?" Offtop took a pull from a new strand he'd just gotten labeled "Jet Fuel".

"Just coolin'...you know, slow motion. Glad to be out here," expressed Khafre dapping Offtop up.

"I hear that," proclaimed Offtop, passing Khafre the blunt.

"Everything a'ight wit'cha?"

"Always, nephew...always!"

"Alrighty."

"Come on in. Let's politic." Offtop waved Khafre in.

"Let's do it," replied Khafre, pulling from the joint as he walked in the house. Once seated in the living room, Khafre noticed a custom-made granite bowl filled with loud, several handmade 1964 Padron cigars, and a bottle of Patron sitting on the table.

"Help ya'self. Give me a minute; I'll be back," said Offtop, disappearing into the back of the house. Khafre poured him a shot and continued smoking the blunt that Offtop gave him.

"Heyyy, baby!" greeted a voice behind Khafre.

When Khafre turned around and saw his auntie CC making her way around the sofa, he immediately thought about everything his father had told him.

"How you doing, Auntie?" replied Khafre, setting the blunt in the ashtray before standing to hug CC's neck. After a warm embrace, CC stepped back and gave Khafre an evaluative look.

"What's up, Auntie?"

"Dang, maaan...you look just like your father. You got that same blood in you too, but from what I was hearing you a lil more dangerous than he was."

"My pops was a legend. I'm just a spoke in a wheel of destiny," Khafre philosophized, looking CC in her eyes.

CC nodded her head in confirmation. "I hear you loud and clear, baby. If you ever need anything, I'on care what it is, you call or come see me. You hear me?"

"Yes ma'am."

"A'ight, bae, give us a minute," Offtop interposed smoothly.

"Okay, I'm out the way. Y'all need anything?"

"We good, bae," assured Offtop.

"You remember what I told you," CC stated, leaving Offtop and Khafre at it.

"I hear you, Auntie," replied Khafre, downing a shot of Patron.

Offtop placed a folder on the table, grabbed the blunt that Khafre had let go out, and re-sparked it. "You gotcha nuts out da pawn shops yet?" asked Offtop, blowing smoke from his nose.

"All night!" replied Khafre, drawing laughter from Offtop.

"It's only right. You deserve that." Offtop hit the blunt again, then poured himself a shot of Patron. "On another note...you thought about what I said the last time you were here?" asked Offtop, doing a shot.

"To tell you the truth, it wasn't nothing to think about. This shit in me, Unc," Khafre retorted briskly.

"Don't I know it. Your father disposed of a lot of problems for me and made a lot of paper doing it too. Since you already in the bidness of disposal. it's only right that I offer you deez contracts."

"I accept," pronounced Khafre pouring another shot.

"We in bidness then. Grab that folder and tell me what'chu think."

Khafre opened the folder and examined the photo of the victim, keeping his face expressionless.

"This bitch-ass nigga, been a pain in my side for years. I hired a private investigator to locate this nigga's whereabouts, and his every move. It's all in that, folder," explained Offtop, sparking another blunt.

Khafre continued to analyze the contents of the folder thoroughly.

After smoking half of the blunt, Offtop put it out. "So, what'chu think?" questioned Offtop.

Khafre closed the folder and set it on the table. "I think this is the sweetest contract a killa could ever be presented with," stated Khafre, voice dripping with malevolence.

Offtop knew that Khafre would accept his first contact with no pressure, and why. Khafre also knew the real reason why Offtop made this contract a priority. It was a silent understanding between them. Offtop poured two shots and handed one to Khafre.

"Wit' that being said, a toast is irrefutable." Both men had their shot glasses in the air. "To contract killing. Salud!"

Killa Kounty 3

CHAPTER 2
YOU TRIPPIN'

"Aye! Aye, bitch, I told you to keep that shit comin'! Why the fuck is my glass empty?" Archie sneered.

"I know you see me serving other customers, nigga!" replied Keyshia seethingly. She was the bartender at BJ's.

"Fuck all that! Refill my shit!" demanded Archie.

"You ain't even paid for the shots you drank yet. I ain't refilling shit!"

"Bitch, you gon' keep my shots coming on yo' dollar or I'ma raid you house hoe. You don't think I know yo' baby daddy trappin' outta yo' house? Huh? Bitch, I'll make one call right now and get yo' shit flipped," Archie threatened, pulling out his phone.

"You need a warrant for that, police-ass nigga!"

"Try me, hoe!" dared Archie, holding his cup out to be refilled.

Keyshia sucked her teeth and refilled Archie's glass.

"My girl," stated Archie with a smirk on his face.

"You're way too cute to be so hostile," asserted a woman's voice seductively.

Archie turned to his right and saw the most stunning white woman he'd ever laid eyes on. He admired the deep arch in her back that complemented her curvy hips and succulent ass.

"Damn! How you doing, Miss Lady?" asked Archie, studying her face.

"I'm fine, but I'd be better if you bought me a drink," she countered sharply, looking Archie up and down intently.

"Not a problem, sunshine. But can I get'cha name first."

"Seems like you've given me one." She laughed, showing her pearly white teeth.

Archie was captivated. Both her smile and tone had an enigmatic quality. "Your beauty reminds me of sunshine," replied Archie nervously.

"Thank you," she said, severely bored with Archie's primitive game. "I'm Hanna."

"Archie."

13

"Nice to meet you, Archie."

"Pleasure is all mine. Aye, Keyshia!" yelled Archie, waving her over.

"Nigga, what?" asked Keyshia peevishly.

Archie went in his pocket and removed a wad of blue hundreds. "This for what I owe you, and, ahhh…what'chu having, beautiful?" "Blue Long Island Iced Tea, please!" exclaimed Hanna.

"Keep me and Miss Lady's drinks coming, please," enunciated Archie, pushing three-hundred dollars towards Keyshia.

Keyshia snatched the money off the bar with a devilish grin on her face. "Oh… Since Snowflake giving you some play, you wanna pay now, huh?"

"Just keep 'em coming," muttered Archie through clenched teeth.

"Yes, sir, officer!" replied Keyshia, refilling Archie's glass, then moving to Hanna's.

"Officer?" questioned Hanna.

"Yeah, I work on the task force," Archie admitted.

"You don't strike me as the type," Hanna stated, moving closer into Archie's space.

"That's the beauty of it. More prevalent for undercover."

"A man of authority. Mmm…" moaned Hanna, putting her hand down Archie pants and whispering in his ear. "Makes my pussy cream." Hanna then licked and kissed his ear, sending chills through Archie's body.

Keyshia cleared her throat and placed Hanna's drink on the bar. "Anything else, Officer?" Keyshia asked sardonically.

Archie waved her away, never looking at her.

"Why don't we skip across the bullshit and get out of here? implored Hanna.

"I'm most definitely wit' dat," assured Archie.

"What do we have here?" asked another woman who was now sitting to the left of Archie.

Archie turned around and saw another beautiful white woman identical to Hanna. "What da fuck?" asked Archie, looking back and forth at both women.

14

"Archie, this is my twin sister, Samantha. Samantha, Archie."

"Damn, how you doing, Samantha?"

"My pussy is jumping so hard right now. You're so fucking, sexy," admitted Samantha

"Yes, lawd!" exclaimed Archie.

"We share everything. Is that a problem for you?" questioned Hanna.

"Not at all!" Archie assured, grabbing his manhood as the thought of fucking two beautiful white women flashed through his mental.

Hanna grabbed both sides of Archie's face and planted a wet kiss on his lips, while Sam quickly slipped a few drops of Visine in Archie's drink.

"One more shot before we leave." Hanna insisted, grabbing her drink to make a toast. Archie grabbed his glass and clinked it against Hanna's. "To a night full of sucking and fucking…and many orgasms," announced Hanna.

Archie wasted no time downing his tainted brandy. Hanna attempted to down her drink, but Samantha intervened. She grabbed Hanna's glass, placed it on the bar, and began kissing her deeply.

"Shit, man!" Archie asserted, smiling from ear to ear, showing all thirty-two gold teeth.

Samantha broke the kiss, then turned to Archie, placing a hand behind his head. "Come here, daddy," said Samantha, pulling him close. She tongue-kissed Archie, then forced Hanna to do the same. The trio continued to swap saliva until Keyshia cleared her throat.

"Y'all hoe asses take this police-ass nigga outta here with all that," Keyshia demanded, knowing that Samantha had put something in Archie's drink. She didn't give a fuck about what Samantha had done. She just didn't want Archie dying in her club.

"No problem," Hanna replied, grabbing Archie by the hand and leading him out of the club.

All the shots Archie had taken were starting to take effect. On the way out of the club, he stumbled past security with a white woman on each arm.

"Damn, Archie, where the party at?" asked Big Rude.

"Stay out my video, po'-ass nigga! Watch dem doors, guard boy!" slurred Archie.

"You got that, Uncle Tom-ass nigga!" replied Big Rude, regretting he even said anything at all.

"Baby, where did you park? Give me your keys." Hanna went in Archie's pockets and removed his keys.

"Aye, hold up. Hold it! Nah, nah, bitch! Don't chu just be goin' in my damn pockets like that, nah!" Archie stated in a drunken stupor, somewhat threatening.

"It's ok, daddy," assured Hanna. "Mama's gonna take good care of you."

A big-ass Kool-Aid smile spread across Archie's face. "You gon' take care of daddy, baby?"

"Yes, me and my sister both." Hanna hit the unlock button on Archie's keychain. The lights came on in a 2022 Jeep Wagoneer truck that Archie had purchased with the money he stole from Khafre's apartment before he went to prison.

"Ooooww, you finna eat that meat off the bone, mama?"

"Gristle and all, daddy," teased Hanna.

"Yes, lawd!" said Archie before Samantha helped him into the front seat, started the truck, and pulled off.

Archie didn't have to give Hanna directions to his beach house on A1A. Due to Offtop's private investigator, that information was alrighty known. When Hanna looked over at Archie, he was slumped in the passenger seat. The eye drops that Samantha put in his drink had taken effect.

***

"A'ight, ladies, I got it from here. Y'all head back to the hotel," Khafre stated, kissing the twins on their cheeks before their departure.

"Call us as soon as you can, daddy," Hanna said with pleading eyes.

"Of course," assured Khafre, closing the door behind them.

16

The familiar sound of Khafre's voice awoke Archie from his comatose-like state. He attempted to move, but realized that he was bound to the bed. He had been stripped naked and laid on his stomach. His legs had been stretched out as far as they could and tied to the bed also. Khafre walked around the bed so Archie could get a clear idea of what he was in for.

"What dey do, homeboy?" asked Khafre, face bearing a sinister grin.

The sight of Khafre caused fear to spread thoughout Archie's body.

"You told me when you sent me to prison that you was gon' fuck my momma! Remember that?" asked Khafre, erasing the smile from his face. "Y'all niggas, make sure all the drapes in this bitch closed," ordered Khafre.

Machi and Hezron moved about, doing as Khafre asked. Archie attempted to turn his head around to see who else was in his house, but his movement was restricted. Samantha had duct-taped Archie's mouth and wrapped it around his head a few times, so his cries for mercy were muffled.

"We good," Machi stated casually.

Khafre wrapped his hands in Archie's dreads and yanked his head back so he could see the devil in his eyes. "Nigga, you killed my pops on an assumption," Khafre stated through clenched teeth. "If my pops killed yo' partna, he would have killed you too, stupid nigga," informed Khafre, spitting in Archie's face and slamming his head into the mattress.

"Quit playin' wit' dis nigga, man," interjected Hezron.

Khafre shot Hezron with a look that stated a warning not to interrupt him again. "I miss my pops. I really do," Khafre admitted, slipping on a pair of gloves. "My pops once told me that there's no better way to mourn a fallen soldier than to pick up the fallen weapon," proclaimed Khafre, picking up a 12-inch PVC pipe and a hammer. "One of y'all, spread dis nigga's cheeks."

"You got a real nigga fucked up! You shoulda kept dem hoes here for that," Hezron declared with a screw face.

"Yeah, you trippin', brah," added Machi.

"Am I? Dis pussy nigga killed my pops…for NOTHIN'! I'ma show y'all how to punish a nigga when he get outta line," pronounced Khafre, pushing a quarter of the PVC pipe into Archie's ass. Archie's eyes grew perceptibly wider as he wailed in pain and confusion. Khafre used the hammer to tap the pipe two more quarters deep, then grabbed two feet of barbed wire from his torture kit.

"You on some other shit!" exclaimed Hezron.

Khafre ignored him and meticulously pushed the wire through the PVC pipe. Once the barbed wire came to a blockade, Khafre removed the PVC pipe, causing Archie's anus to close around the barbed wire. Archie squirmed and wailed to no avail. Khafre snatched the barbed wire from Archie's ass, pulling some of his intestines out with it.

"You a twisted nigga, fam," Hezron stated, caught off-guard by Khafre's heinousness. Machi just stood observing apathetically.

As Archie pissed and released bloody fecal matter, Khafre gazed at Hezron with a quizzical expression, face tightening with emotion. "Dis bitch-ass nigga killed Pops and sent me to prison for five years! Do you know what da fuck I had to go through in gladiator camp? Huh? You ever felt hopeless? I'm talkin' ten, fifteen niggas trying to kill you every day! Fuck dis nigga, fam!" The edge in Khafre's tone cut across Hezron's and Machi's consciousness.

"Calm down, Cuz, I'm wit'chu," assured Hezron.

"Damn, my nigga, act like it."

"You right, fam," said Hezron, walking around the bed. "Dis for my uncle, and fucking wit' my pops, nigga!" exclaimed Hezron, pulling a FN-502 with a suppressor from his hoodie and planted three holes in the back of Archie's head, sending a reddish-pink mist into the air. Machi followed suit, pulling the same caliber from his hoodie. With no words, he drilled two more holes in what was left of Archie's head. Khafre removed a MP5 with a silencer from his bag and peppered Archie's body with hot ones from head to toe.

"Bitch-ass nigga! Y'all come on. We gon' put dis nigga's truck in Taylor's creek."

CHAPTER 3
I'M WIT'CHU

A week later, Khafre picked the money up from Offtop. The contract for Archie was for 100 bands, and even though Machi and Hezron didn't want any of it, Khafre still gave them twenty-five apiece. He was now pulling into Tillman's Bar-Be-Cue. Tillman's was a black-owned establishment that for some odd reason was more frequented by whites than blacks. He started with one grill, selling drugs outside of the clubs and on the side of US-1 Highway. Tillman's became a major franchise.

Khafre entered Tillman's and spotted his mother, Shantell, sitting in a booth alone.

"What's up, Mama?" Khafre approached the booth.

Shantell stood and hugged Khafre's neck, smiling all the while, happy so see him.

"Hey, Mama's baby," greeted Shantell.

Khafre kissed Shantell on her cheek and had a seat across from her. "Sorry I'm a li'l late. I had to handle, a li'l something."

"It's okay, baby. I'm just happy to see you."

"Hi, I'm Jade. I'll be your server today. Can I start you guys off with something to drink, or are you ready to place an order?" Jade asked briskly.

Khafre took one look at Jade and was captivated by her beauty. A beauty that he knew enamored men and devastated women. Jade only stood 4'9", but her body was that of a dancer. Her skin was a blemish-free and coal black, and her teeth snow white. Khafre never got into women that wore low haircuts, but the way that Jade styled it with poise that exuded femininity was alluring. Her designer spectacles gave her a weird, geeky, sexy type vibe, and Khafre wanted to see what that was about.

"Um….yes, I'll have the five-rib dinner with mac-n-cheese, baked beans, and the buttery parmesan Texas toast. I'll have an iced tea with that," said Shantell.

"Okay, and you, sir?" asked Jade. She secretly admired how handsome Khafre was.

"Ahh…to be honest, what I have an appetite for does not seem to be on the menu," Khafre pronounced while studying the menu.

"And what is that, sir?"

"Fillet-mign*you*," replied Khafre, gazing deeply into her enchanting light-brown pupils.

Jade smiled, taken aback by Khafre's wittiness. "Neologism. That was cute," she admitted.

"Neo-who?" Khafre curiously asked.

"Neologism. A new word or meaning for an established word," informed Jade, using the tip of her index fingers to push her frames back in place

"Beauty and brains. I love it."

"Boy, stop flirting with that girl and order your food. You'll get her fired," stated Shantell.

"Hatin' don't look good on you, Ma," Khafre replied jokingly.

"Boy, whatever! I'm hungry. Order your food, please!" cried Shantell.

"I'ma have the same thang she ordered."

"Okay, your food will be ready shortly. Welcome to Tillmans, " Jade said before walking off.

"Mama, when you see me saucin', please don't disturb my drip."

Shantell shook her head, smiling. "Boy you just like yo' father."

"Speaking of my father…You still got the money, he came home wit' from the feds?"

"Yeah, I got it put up for you. Why?" Shantell asked.

"I think I wanna open up a business."

"That's fine. You know what'chu wanna do?"

"I got a idea, but I'ma revisit this conversation when I get it figured out."

"That's good. I'm glad you're taking steps towards positive things." Jade approached and placed their meals on the table. "Sorry I didn't bring your drinks first. I'll be back in a minute with your iced teas," said Jade.

"That's okay, baby," Shantell assured before she left again.

Shantell wasted no time devouring her ribs. Khafre just nibbled on the famous Texas toast.

"Mama, I wanted to talk to you about something important."

"I'm here," replied Shantell, licking barbeque sauce from her fingers. Jade came back and placed their drinks on the table.

"Once again, I'm sorry about the drinks," Jade stated.

"You cool, beautiful," affirmed Khafre.

Jade wrote her number on an ordering ticket and slid it to Khafre. "Call me. We'll discuss more about neologism," proclaimed Jade, smiling before walking off.

"What'chu wanted to talk 'bout?" questioned Shantell.

"You remember that detective who sent me to prison?"

"Yeah, you're talking about Archie. I seen him on the news. Somebody killed him."

"He killed Pops," stated Khafre.

Shantell stopped chewing and took a sip from her iced tea before replying. "How do you know that?" asked Shantell, confused.

"I was there. I seen him."

"Why would he kill your father?"

"He thought Pops killed his partner."

Shantell sat and gazed at Khafre in a dubious state. "Who told you this?"

"Never mind that, Mama. Now you know I don't hide anything from you. Right?"

"Right. We don't do that."

"I'm the one killed that nigga," Khafre stated with an air of dismissal. The familiar look in Khafre's eyes let her know that he was graveyard serious.

"Khafre, you just got out of prison. I understand you avenging your father's death, but a detective?" Shantell implored, concerned.

"When it comes to protecting what I love, anybody can get it. Especially when it's a ticket on your head."

"A ticket? What'chu mean, Khafre?"

"I'm a contract killa, mama."

"Contract killa? So you telling me somebody paid you to kill a cop?"

Khufu

"Affirmative. He killed Pops anyway. Feels like a win-win to me."

"Oh lawd, have mercy Jesus," sighed Shantell.

"I'on really wanna hear that, Mama. This what it is. Deez contracts, brangin' in a lot of money. I need to know if you wit' me or not?"

Shantell took a deep breath and exhaled before replying. "You my only son, of course I'm wit'chu."

"Thank you, Mama. I love you."

"I love you too, Khafre."

CHAPTER 4
BE CAREFUL

"How my girls doing?" Khafre asked Hanna and Samantha, who were Facetiming with him as he sat parked outside of the Brown Store.

"We miss you, daddy!" the twins sang in unison.

"As you should," replied Khafre, voice dripping with nonchalance. "Listen, it's imperative that I see y'all. When can we meet up?

"Well, we're taking a trip to Cape Elizabeth with our mom in two days. We'll be back in two weeks, daddy," proclaimed Hanna.

"Da fuck y'all going to Maine for?"

"Just something we always wanted to do," laughed Samantha.

"Why is it imperative that we see you?" questioned Hanna.

"I wanted to discuss a li'l bidness proposal."

"What did you have in mind, baby?" Samantha implored.

"It's a lot of rich white folks, wit' yachts and shit in Naples?"

"Too many. Why? You want us to set a few of them up for you, daddy?" asked Hanna.

"That wouldn't be a bad idea, but no, nothing like that. I wanna start a yacht cleaning bidness."

"That's a great idea, Khafre. We can help you build your clientele!" exclaimed Samantha.

"Exactly what I wanted to hear. Listen, I'm finna handle something. Y'all call me soon as y'all get back."

"Okay daddy," the twins said in unison.

"Show me that pussy before I go."

Both Hanna and Samantha pulled their boy shorts to the side happily.

"Ooowwee! Pink salmon. I love it." The twins giggled at Khafre's remark.

"You're so silly. See you when we get back," said Hanna.

"Yeah, yeah," replied Khafre, hanging up the phone.

He then got out of his car and headed into the Brown Store. The smell of fresh chicken gizzards and liver clouded Khafre's nostrils.

"Wholly!"

"Yeah, buddy, one second!" exclaimed Wholly, pulling the gizzards from the grease, never looking up at Khafre.

"Let a nigga get five-dollars' worth of gizzards and a pound of weed," clowned Khafre.

"Hey buddy, no——!" Wholly's words were cut short when he looked up and saw Khafre smiling. "Khafre?"

"What up wit' it?"

"Oh my goodness. You look different with your hair cut. Welcome home, my friend," pronounced Wholly, reaching across the counter to shake Khafre's hand.

"It feels good to be here," replied Khafre.

"If you need anything, my friend, let me know."

"You can start by giving me a box of dem, gizzards," Khafre asserted, chuckling.

"Okay, buddy," retorted Wholly, grabbing a Styrofoam box to put the gizzards in.

"You rented the apartment when I was gone?"

"No, your mother keeps it paid up. I have an extra key. You can go check it out, if you'd like," Wholly offered.

"Yeah, I'ma slide up there," Khafre replied.

Wholly went in his back pocket and handed Khafre the key. "You can keep it. Let me know if you need anything, buddy," said Wholly, pushing the box of gizzards towards Khafre.

"Appreciate it," replied Khafre loading his gizzards with hot sauce, ketchup, and jalapeno peppers.

"Don't worry about the gizzards…on the house."

"Bet that up. I'ma get wit'chu later!" exclaimed Khafre, grabbing his food and heading out of the store.

Right when Khafre opened the door, someone was coming in. They both stopped and locked eyes for a few seconds.

"What da fuck is up, nigga?" asked Khafre.

"You already know, my nigga. I'm out'chere!"

"Mothafuckin' Sito! When you touched down?"

"I've been out three days now," replied Sito.

"Good to see you! Bitch, wassup? You need something?" asked Khafre.

"I been home for three days, and I done already touched two niggas. I'm straight, but shid... If you still wanna shoot me something, I ain't gon' turn it down."

Khafre went in his pocket and counted out two-thousand. "Here, nigga." Khafre handed Sito the money.

"Good, lookin', my nigga. Shid, lock my number in."

Khafre pulled his phone out and locked Sito's number in. "Who you got in the car, wit'chu?" questioned Khafre, looking in the Kia that Sito pulled up in.

"Oh I got that hoe Chocolate in there wit' me," Sito declared with a smile on his face.

"Chocolate?"

"Yeah, wassup?" asked Sito, giving Khafre a quizzical expression.

"Mannn...be careful wit' that hoe, brah. She be wit' dem niggas on the other side," warned Khafre.

"She ain't no hoe, brah, and I ain't worried 'bout no niggas. I can handle mine," declared Sito.

There was a slight change in the wind. Khafre could sense a light tone of aggression in Sito's voice. Khafre knew firsthand that Chocolate had the capability of controlling a man's thoughts and emotions with her pussy and mouth if that man was weak-minded. It was said and known around the city that Chocolate was setting niggas up to be killed. That's the main reason Khafre cut her off years ago.

"A'ight, my nigga. Breathe. I'm just looking out for you, but you say you got it, you got it then."

"I'ma fuck with'chu later, my nigga," Sito stated, dapping Khafre up before walking into the store.

Khafre took another glance at Chocolate, who smiled at him. He shook his head and walked to the back of the store, making a mental note of Sito's weakness: pussy!

When Khafre made it back to his apartment, he noticed that it was spotless. Shantell had kept it clean and left the decor the same, since she knew that Niya was responsible for it. The last time Khafre was in his apartment was when he'd came home and found his place trashed by Archie's break in. Archie had taken a couple hunnid grand from under Khafre's mattress. The thought of it made Khafre head to his bedroom. He saw that Shantell had gotten him a bigger and better mattress and had filled his closet with all the latest designers. Khafre smiled, pulled out his phone, and called his mother.

"Hello?" answered Shantell.

"I love you, Mama."

"Boy, what'chu done did now?" Shantell implored, drawing laughter from Khafre.

"Nothing, Ma. I'm inside my apartment. I just wanted to tell you thank you, and I love you."

"You welcome, baby, and I love you too. How did you get in?"

"Wholly."

"Oh, okay. I was gonna surprise you, but I guess it all worked out. You like it?"

"Love it. Where you at?"

"I'm having a drink with a friend."

"You wit' a nigga?" asked Khafre somewhat threateningly, now drawing laughter from Shantell.

"And if I was,? Boy, I'm grown."

"Where you at?"

"I'm with a friend...girl. Golly, man!"

"What does she look like? Put me in the car with her, Ma."

"Boy, bye!" Click!

Moments after Shantell hung the phone up, Khafre's phone rang.

"Yeah, what's up?"

"I got something for you," stated Offtop.

"I'm in da wind," replied Khafre.

"Already!"

CHAPTER 5
SUIT UP

Headed to Fort Lauderdale, Khafre got off on exit Sunrise and headed west over the bridge past Franklin Park. Once he made it to Lauder Hill County, he made a right on 55th, headed to 19th Street, and pulled into a Quick Pick gas station. Khafre spotted the old 2004 F150 and parked next to it. After putting one in the head of his Sar 9x9 mm, Khafre hopped out and approached the truck. The sound of the doors being unlocked prompted Khafre to opened the door and hop in.

"What's up, brah! I'm Jack." Jack stuck his fist out.

"What up?" replied Khafre, ready to cut past the small talk and put in work.

"Offtop say you the real deal," pronounced Jack, putting the truck in gear and pulling off.

"We ain't gotta do all that. Just show me where to demonstrate at."

"Calm down, li'l homie, I'ma lace you up. Let me make this li'l pit stop right quick. That okay wit'chu?"

"Do you!" exclaimed Khafre.

Jack headed to J-N-I, liquor store and grabbed a bottle of Rosé and Patron. Sitting in the parking lot, Jack cracked the seal on the Patron and poured himself a cup.

"Pour you a cup, brah," Jack insisted.

"I'm good."

"Man...get in the vibe while I lace you up on this pussy nigga."

"Fuck it." stated Khafre, fixing himself a cup of straight Patron. After downing his first cup, Khafre started to loosen up and relax. Once Jack noticed this, he pulled off and headed to Franklin Park.

"Right now we are in Franklin Park. This the opp side." Khafre nodded his head up and down, letting Jack know that he was listening. "The nigga I want out the way, he from Franklin. This pussy-ass nigga Rome call me and say he gotta play for a brick of flocka. He supposed to be my nigga, so, I give the nigga the work, right? How 'bout, this crab-ass nigga run off wit' my shit."

Khufu

"Cutthroat." Khafre downed another cup.

"I know, right? So, I call the nigga and ask 'em wassup? How 'bout this nigga beat me getting mad about my own shit."

"Nall?" clowned Khafre.

"Yeaaah, man! Shit crazy, man? So fast forward, right. I'm coming outta Club Troy's one night, over there on 31st and Sunrise. Soon as I make it to my whip, the nigga came outta nowhere and give it to me. Hit me ten times, but I bounced back like good dope, ya hear me!

"Damn," Khafre ad-libbed.

"Yeaahh, man! See, the nigga know how I get down, so he got me before I can get him."

"Smart man," stated Khafre.

"Not smart enough. He should have hit me in the head," exclaimed Jack creeping past an establishment known as The Friendly Store. "See the nigga in the blue collar shirt?"

"Yeah."

"That's him," declared Jack, pulling into some low-income apartments called The Greens that sat directly behind The Friendly Store.

"Say less. Keep the truck running," Khafre advised, getting out of the truck, pulling his Red Sox fitted cap low. He jumped the wall that separated the apartments and was now behind the store. Khafre pulled his banga and rounded the store. Everybody saw Khafre except Rome, who had his back towards Khafre, telling his homies war stories. Rome wondered why his homies started backing up slowly.

"This shit ain't fa y'all!" stated Khafre as he upped his tool.

When Rome turned around, Khafre hit him twice in the midsection, dropping him. Rome's homies scattered, leaving him for dead. His eyes grew in size when he saw Khafre standing over him.

"That boy Jack sends his regards."

Boc! Boc! Boc! Khafre put three rounds in Rome's face, then sprinted back to the wall behind the store. He leaped over it and hopped back in the truck with Jack.

"You got 'em?" Jack asked, hyped up.

28

"Don't insult my gangsta."

Jack smiled. "My man," said Jack, driving by the store to see Khafre's work. He saw Rome stretched out with a civilian squatting next to him.

"Yeeeeah! Look at'chu, pussy nigga," stated Jack, getting on the gas and heading back to Deep Side.

Back at the Quick Pick, Jack pulled next to Khafre's rental car and put his truck in park.

"Listen, I like how you handled that. If you available, I got another one for you. I'll get'cha a room, then call you later wit' the play. It's on you."

"How much?" asked Khafre.

"Thirty."

"I accept. But let me ask you something."

"Wassup, li'l homie?"

"Why you ain't hit da nigga, ya'self?" Khafre asked, looking Jack in his eyes.

"I'm a boss, li'l homie. I ain't gotta get my hands dirty. I put checks on niggas' heads."

"That nigga hit'chu ten times. Sounds like it was worth, getting ya hands dirty to me!" Khafre exclaimed "Plus you still in da same whip as me. That makes you an accessory."

"You right, li'l brah, but at the end of the day, that nigga no longer wit' us. Ya hear me?"

"I'm just here for a check," replied Khafre.

"I hear you. Aye, I just came across a gang of loud. I'm talking about pounds of that shit. You hustle?" asked Jack, diverting the conversation.

"Right now, I'm just smacking shit, brah. So, if you don't mind, show me where the room at. I need a li'l rest."

"Say no mo', lil home."

***

After taking a shower, Khafre lay alone in his hotel room and dialed Jade's number from a burner phone. She picked up on the third ring.

"This is Jade, who's calling?"

"How are you doin', beautiful? Dis Khafre."

"Umm, sorry, I don't know anyone by that name."

"I have a distinct voice, so I know you know who I am."

"Sounds familiar, but....nope. Can't say that I know you."

"You were supposed to give me neologism 101.Remember?"

"Oh, Mr. Neologism, took you long enough to call. How are you?"

"I'm a busy man, but since you a li'l vibrant thang, I made time for you. I'm coolin', thanks for askin'."

"Okay then, Q-Tip. I guess I should feel special, huh?"

"You better know it," replied Khafre, voice dripping with arrogance.

Jade laughed before replying. "I can see now, you too much."

"What'chu doing? Well...what were you doin', before I called?"

"Reading Harry Potter. Don't judge me."

"Harry Potter? Oooww...I got myself a li'l sexy geek. Dis gon' be interesting."

"What'chu mean, you got? We never discussed me being yours," Jade retorted seductively.

"It's inevitable, baby girl."

"Mmm!" moaned Jade

"What?"

"Don't call me that."

"Why not?"

"You just made my pussy wet," admitted Jade.

"Thank you, God!" exclaimed Khafre.

"For what?"

"I got a sexy, geeky freak!" Khafre drew more laughter from Jade.

"When can I see you?" questioned Jade. Khafre's phone beeped.

"I'm out of town on bidness. Soon as I get back, I'm in ya chest."

"Okay. I'ma hold you to that."

"I'ma call you later. I gotta important incoming call."

"That's fine, handsome."

"A'ight," replied Khafre, clicking over.

"Yeah?"

"Suit up," declared Jack.

Khufu

CHAPTER 6
THE OFFICE

Jack pulled into the Days Inn parking lot in a Ford Taurus and put the car in park. He then called Khafre on his burner phone. Khafre noticed that his phone started ringing as soon as the Ford Taurus pulled in. He knew it was Jack. So instead of answering , he slid from behind a van and knocked on Jacks passenger window, startling him. ,Jack unlocked the doors and Khafre hopped in.

"Boy, I see you light on ya toes," stated Jack. "I'm gon' start calling you Tiptoe."

Khafre chuckled.

"Oh yeah? You think so?" Jack showed all thirty-two gold teeth.

"Man… What up? What da lick, read? I'm ready to wet something and get back to da city!" exclaimed Khafre with a trace of impatience.

"Oh, you in a rush? You know, that's how mistakes get made, rushing and shit."

"Speaking of rushin', you got my money?"

"Yeah, I got it."

"I'ma need that up front, homie," Khafre declared.

"You ain't saying nothing. Get it from under yo' seat."

Khafre pulled his pistol and turned it with his right hand, pointing it at Jack as he reached under his seat and grabbed a brown paper bag. He glanced in the bag and saw that it was on point.

"Damn, li'l homie, you robbing me?" questioned Jack, perplexed.

Khafre set his pistol on his lap before speaking. "Nothin' like that, my nigga. I done seen niggas get played like that."

"Like what?" asked Jack, still confused.

"You tell me, reach under da seat, then blow my shit off. I done seen it," explained Khafre.

"I'on do bidness like, that li'l homie," Jack pronounced, putting the car in gear and pulling off.

"I just met'chu, my nigga."

"You right. I see you military-minded. I like that," Jack admitted.

"Comin' from where I'm from, ain't no other way to be."

"I heard how y'all doin' all that killin' in Fort Pierce."

"Killa Kounty."

"That's what dey say," said Jack, pulling into a club called The Office. Jack found a parking spot, cut the car off, and gave Khafre the rundown.

"See dis nigga right here?" said Jack, showing Khafre a picture of the nigga he wanted dead.

"Yeah."

"Dis the nigga C.B. This the nigga we finna get."

"We?"

"Yeah, I wanna get in on dis one. Dis pussy nigga the one who introduced me, to the nigga Rome. He gets it too."

"Already," replied Khafre.

"I got a hoe on him, working his dumb ass, as we speak. Come on, let's go in, and bring ya strap. I know the security guard."

Khafre took the money out of the brown bag. It was ten stacks for each rubber band. Khafre put twenty bands in his front left pocket and ten in his right. He then tucked his pistol on his waist and exited the vehicle. Once at the front entrance, Khafre saw an attractive woman who favored Snow Black, an Instagram model.

"Cookie, wassup, girl? You a'ight tonight?" asked Jack.

"Heyyy Jack, I'm alright. How 'bout yourself?"

"Can't complain," pronounced Jack, paying the entry fee for him and Khafre.

"I heard that. Who you got wit'cha? He is cute," Cookie flirted.

"Hey, my mans, let me pat'cha down right quick. I stepped off for a minute, that's my bad," the security guard pronounced.

"He wit' me, he Gucci," Jack stated, waving Khafre forward.

"Give your friend, my number, Jack," asserted Cookie, eyeing Khafre.

"I got'cha," assured Jack, entering the club.

Khafre had never been to a strip club. He was amazed at the variety of beautiful women. There was ass, pussy, and titties everywhere. Khafre followed Jack to the V.I.P. section, taking in the ambience. Not long after being seated, Khafre noticed the man from the picture on Jack's phone. It was C.B. at another table in V.I.P., being worked like Jack had said. He glanced in Khafre's and Jack's direction, but did not show much interest in caring. Jack acted as if he didn't see C.B. and ordered bottles of Rosé and Patron. He ordered a few dances and threw a couple thousand dollars as they laid on C.B. Jack had drunk nearly the whole bottle of Rosé by himself, while Khafre refused to drink at all. Khafre figured that C.B. had to have heard about Rome getting smacked in front of the Friendly Store. He felt like C.B. was trying to rock Jack to sleep by acting as if everything was Gucci.

"Why you ain't drankin', brah?" Jack asked, still throwing money.

"Gotta stay on point."

Moments later, C.B. got up and was being led out of the club by a beautiful Haitian woman.

"Got 'em," Jack stated, smiling.

After sitting in the club twenty more minutes, Jack and Khafre left and headed to the hotel. The reason Jack chose this rundown hotel was because it had no cameras. He fired up a cigarette and waited on a text message from the Haitian woman who was with C.B.

"Even though I paid you, brah, I appreciate this shit. Ya hear me?"

"Already," Khafre replied. His phone rang seconds later. "Yah?" answered Khafre. "You sho'? Shid...say less." As soon as Khafre hung up the phone, Jack got a message.

"This is her right here, brah. Showtime," Jack announced, putting the cigarette out.

Boc!

Khafre put a hole in Jack's head, splattering blood and brain matter about the driver's window. Khafre wiped the door handle, got out, wiped the outside door handle, then traversed to his rental. He got on I-95 and headed back to Fort Pierce.

The phone call he had received was from Offtop. It had just come to Offtop's attention that Jack had sent someone to rob one of his plugs. The robbery went bad and Offtop's plug died in the process. He ordered Khafre to smack Jack.

CHAPTER 7
SOME STREET SHIT

"Heyyy, Auntie's baby. How you been?" CC asked, excited to see her nephew.

Khafre hugged CC's neck before replying. "I just been maining, Auntie," Khafre said, stepping inside.

"Maining?" questioned CC, confused.

"Maintaining."

"Oh, okay. That shit went over my head. I'm getting old," stated CC, laughing, closing the door behind her.

"You gotta stay in da loop, Auntie."

"Y'all millennials are crazy as hell. Go 'head, yo' uncle in there."

Khafre made his way to the living room. Offtop had a money machine and a stack of money on the table.

"What up wit' it, Unc?" greeted Khafre, dapping Offtop up before taking a seat next to him.

"You see what it is. Fire one of dem blunts up," Offtop stated, loading the machine with more bills.

Khafre grabbed a lighter and put flame to a pre-rolled blunt. After taking a deep toke, Khafre coughed repeatedly and started to drool. Offtop laughed, then reached for the blunt.

"Pass that shit, and fix you something to drink."

Khafre passed the blunt and poured a shot of Remy. "What that is?" asked, Khafre downing the shot of Remy.

"I put wax on the blunt before I rolled it wit' birthday cake," proclaimed Offtop before hitting the blunt. He was so used to smoking wax that he just coughed once and loaded the money machine again. This time when the machine beeped, Offtop removed the money and handed it to Khafre.

"Here, that's you. Sixty bands." Offtop poured himself a shot.

"Alrighty," replied Khafre, grabbing the money.

"Listen, I'm always keeping it 50/20's wit'cha. Every time, I give you a contract, I take my percentage off the top. That's my finder's fee."

"I overstand that, Unc," assured Khafre, now galvanized from the weed and Remy.

"I'm just lacing up cuz I enjoy doing good bidness. Now the original contract was for the sixty. I took my fifty percent off the top, but once I got word that Jack got my plug hit, I put his own money on his head," explained Offtop, downing a shot of Remy.

"Damn! How da hell he knew who yo' plug was?"

"We been doin' bidness for years. A few months ago, my plug threw me a party at City Hall. I made so much money for him, I guess he wanted to show his appreciation. Anyway, I invited dis nigga Jack to the party, since he was doing good bidness. He peeped who my plug was and had his people lay on him while we were at the party. One of his people gave him up for a pound of weed," pronounced Offtop, laughing.

"Ain't no more righteous left, Unc."

"It's a part of the game," Offtop declared, re-lighting the blunt.

"So, I'm curious."

"'Bout what?" questioned Offtop, blowing smoke from his nose.

"What'chu gon' do 'bout da nigga who gave Jack up?"

"It's already been taken care of," Offtop assured as his phone began to ring. "Give me a minute. Hello? A'ight, I'll be there."

"Everything, good Unc?"

"Yeah. I gotta move around for a minute. Yo' cousins back there. I'll be back in a li'l bit," Offtop stated, grabbing his keys and heading for the door.

Khafre fired up another blunt, then headed towards the back of the house, where he could hear Hezron talking shit to Machi.

"Hold me down while I grab da jewelry, nigga! Fuck is you doing?" exclaimed Hezron.

"Nigga, I'm trying grab some jewelry too!" said Machi.

When Khafre entered Hezron's room, he saw that they had their backs turned to the door, playing PS5.

"Fuck is up?" yelled Khafre.

All in one swift motion, Hezron grabbed his pistol from his lap and upped it on Khafre.

"Squeeze, nigga," taunted Khafre.

"You don't want that," declared Hezron. "I heard you in there, talking to my ops," Hezron admitted.

"What up, Cuz?" greeted Machi.

"What's up wit' it?" Khafre replied, walking in the room, dapping both of his cousins up.

"We in here on this Payday," pronounced Machi, referring to the game that they were playing.

"I'm saying…I want y'all to slide somewhere wit' me."

"What'chu tryin' to do?" implored Hezron.

"I'm finna slide to Arkbar's shop and get tatted," Khafre said.

"Shid, we ain't doin' shit. We'll slide. We can smoke in there?" questioned Hezron.

"Yeah."

"Machi, don't forget to load yo' shit," advised Hezron.

"Nigga, do I ever?"

***

Arkbar was a Miami native that moved to Fort Pierce and opened a tattoo shop on Avenue D dubbed Hood Ink. He was a proficient tattoo artist who provide reasonable prices and stayed open 24 hours a day. When Khafre walked into the shop with Hezron and Machi behind him, he noticed Chocolate with two of her friends, Crystal and Amber. The two were looking at tattoo books, trying to decide on what they wanted. All three women knew Khafre was a killer, so the energy in the shop shifted upon his arrival. Chocolate shifted in her seat and crossed her legs to contain the thumping sensation in her pussy. She bit her lip before speaking.

"Heyyy, Khafre," greeted Chocolate seductively.

Khafre just nodded his head and kept it moving. He recognized Crystal, who was a true hustler, and Amber, who was a pill poppin' animal.

"What's up, Khafre?" asked Crystal.

"What dey do?" Khafre replied as he approached Arkbar, who was at his tattoo station smoking one. Hezron and Machi sat next to Crystal and Amber, then began to roll up blunts.

"What can I do for you, lil homie?" asked Arkbar.

"I want three portraits and three teardrops."

"Let me see the portraits."

Khafre pulled his phone out and showed Arkbar pictures of Shenida, Nilya, and his father.

"I know him. I did all of his tattoos," stated Arkbar, pointing at Baby G photo.

"That's my pops. He got killed by a pussy nigga," Khafre voiced seethingly.

"Yeah, I heard," Arkbar replied with empathy.

"Trust me, it's all good," Khafre stated, giving Arkbar a familiar look that stated he had avenged his father.

"Yo' father was a fucking legend, my nigga! I'll tell you what. I'ma do the portrait of ya father for free, then the other ones half price, my nigga."

"I'm feelin' that. Let's do it."

Hezron walked in, handed Khafre a blunt, then headed back to the waiting area. Khafre removed his shirt, fired his blunt up, and laid down while Arkbar went to work. In the waiting area, Machi and Hezron were smoking while being harassed by Crystal and Amber.

"Boy, I know you," Amber stated to Hezron.

"You don't know me. You trippin'!"

"Yes, I do. You that boy who was in that video wit' Khafre. Y'all went live at the graveyard."

"I'on know what'chu talkin' 'bout. Like I said, hoe, you tripping!" Hezron retorted, taking a toke on his blunt.

"Boy, whatever. Let me hit yo' blunt."

"You won't put'cha meat grippers on dis," clowned Hezron. taking another pull from his blunt.

"Well, let me put 'em on you, then," Amber retorted, causing Hezron to choke on the reefer smoke.

Machi and Crystal laughed.

"Shid, shoot me ya number. I'll let'chu chew me later," Hezron declared, brushing the ashes from his designer jeans.

"Nall, nigga, I wanna eat that dick up now. Snatch it out. I wanna see it!" Amber exclaimed, biting her bottom lip.

"Whoa!" added Machi.

"Hoe, you tweaking!" Hezron said. looking at Amber dubiously.

The door to the shop opened and two niggas walked in wearing R.I.P. shirts. Hezron and Machi immediately stopped talking and got on point. Arkbar had clients from both sides of town, so wasn't no telling who might show up. The two dudes walked straight to the back where Arkbar and Khafre were.

"What's good, y'all?" asked Arkbar, looking up for a brief moment before continuing to work on Khafre's ink. "I'ma be booked for a while. Y'all might wanna come back tomorrow."

Khafre looked up and saw Lotto and Smoke ice grilling him. He then noticed that they were wearing shirts that read R.I.P. Kurt.

"Hold up, Arkbar." Khafre stated, rising up to face whatever he had coming. He inhaled smoke from his blunt, then blew smoke in the faces of Kurt's comrades.

"Kill me, respect, or leave me the fuck alone!" Khafre declared.

Smoke flinched, causing Khafre to throw a right hook that landed on Smoke's chin and dropped him. Lotto attempted to sucker punch Khafre, but he was already weaving Lotto's right and he countered with a right uppercut, dropping Lotto next to Smoke. Khafre hit his joint, then dumped the ashes on his opps.

Click-clack! Hezron and Machi were now standing over Smoke and Lotto guns down.

"Not in my shop, my nigga. Catch dem niggas outside," pronounced Arkbar.

"Don't hit 'em. Take everything dem niggas got and give it to dem hoes in there," ordered Khafre.

Machi and Hezron took Smoke's and Lotto's jewelry and money, then escorted them out of the shop. They then divided everything between the women.

"Y'all is crazy!" voiced Crystal.

Amber gave Hezron her number while Chocolate walked out to where Khafre was.

"Khafre, you okay?" Chocolate asked, concerned.

"Go on 'bout ya bidness, my nigga," warned Khafre.

"It's like that? Damn!" whined Chocolate.

"I'on fuck wit'chu. You poison."

"What was that about?" asked Arkbar.

"Some street shit."

CHAPTER 8
YOU KILLED SOMEBODY?

It had been two weeks since the incident at Arkbar's shop. Khafre thought he was being followed, but every time he grabbed his pistol and pulled over, the vehicle would just drive right by him.

He came to the conclusion that the weed was making him paranoid. After discussing his plans of starting a yacht business with his mother, Khafre had her start an LLC in her name. He decided to call it Royal Yacht Cleansing. Even though Khafre was still taking contracts, Shantell expressed how elated she was that he was making an effort towards something positive. Khafre was now headed to Jade's, when his phone rang.

"Talk to me," answered Khafre.

"Heyyy, baby. How are you?'" asked Hanna gracefully.

"I'm coolin', what up?"

"I'm calling to let you know, that I started a business page for Royal Yacht Cleansing and that you have your first client this weekend. He's actually a friend of the family. You'll like him; he's cool. And before you even ask, he knows that you're black." Khafre chuckled.

"Okay, that's my girl. You did good. How much did you price this job for?"

"Well, since everybody with yachts down here are rich snobs, we'll charge them fifty dollars per foot. The yacht that we're cleaning this weekend is a one-hundred footer, so that'll be five-thousand in one day, babe."

"That's a nice bit of change. I want you and Samantha to clean in bikinis."

"We're ahead of you on that one, daddy," laughed Hanna.

"Tell Samantha I said what up."

"She can hear you, babe."

"Hi daddy!" yelled Samantha.

"What up wit' it? You miss daddy dick?"

"You have no fucking idea!" cried Samantha.

"I gotcha, ma. Look, I'm finna pull up on something, so I'ma get at y'all."

"Bye!"

Khafre hung up and made a left on 32nd Street and Avenue M in the projects known as V-Side, or Vietnam. He noticed that a Chevy Impala with heavily-tinted windows had been following him since his phone call with the twins. Khafre clutched his Springfield Hellcat 9mm, made another quick left on Avenue L, put his car in park, and hopped out. As soon as the Impala attempted to turn the corner, Khafre let loose, peppering the driver's door with Honey Badger rounds. Instead of turning the corner, the driver turned the wheel back straight, swerving in an attempt to escape death.

Boc! Boc! Boc! Boc! Boc!

"Yeaaaah, nigga, yeah!" Khafre yelled in between squeezes.

Boc! Boc! Boc!

The driver of the Impala almost lost control of the vehicle, but managed to slip away. Khafre hopped back in his whip and made a right on 29th and L. He then made a right on 29th and Avenue I, creeping until he reached 32nd again. The Impala was nowhere in sight. He turned into the driveway of Jade's apartment and pulled around the back. Jade was in the kitchen cooking dinner, so she saw Khafre pull behind her apartment and hop out. She met him at the back door and let him in.

"Hey handsome."

"What's good, beautiful? "Khafre retorted, grabbing Jade and pulling her close like he'd known her forever.

"You mind tellin' me, why did you pull to the back door of my apartment?" Jade implored with her hands on her hips.

"Outta respect for what'chu got going on, I pulled in da back," lied Khafre.

"What I got going on?"

"Yeah. I'on want'cha li'l boyfriend to see my shit parked in ya driveway. He might be on some hoe shit, and pour sugar in my tank or key my shit up. Then, I'ma have to kill his ass."

"First off, I'm single. Second, why is you lying to me?"

"'Bout what?"

"So you ain't have nothing to do with them gunshots I just heard?"

"Nall," Khafre lied again.

Jade patted Khafre down and felt the gun in his right pocket. "Give it here. Let me see it," Jade demanded.

Curious as to what she was going to do with the gun, Khafre removed his pistol and handed it to her. Jade sniffed the barrel of the gun, shook her head, then handed Khafre back his pistol. She then headed back in the kitchen to check on her food.

"What?" asked Khafre as he followed behind her, smiling.

"I got five brothers," Jade stated, taking the lid off her pot to her beef neckbones.

"And?"

"And…just 'cause I read Harry Potter, that doesn't mean I don't know what it is out here. I'm not green. That pistol was fired, like moments ago. Tsss! How we gon' start something, and you are already lying?"

Khafre rubbed his hand over his face before replying. "You right, ma. I just figured the less you know, the better."

"So who was it?" Jade questioned, closing the lid on her pot and turning to face Khafre.

"I don't know. Some niggas was trailing my car, making every turn I made, so, I hopped out and gave it to 'em."

"You killed somebody?"

"Not dis time," proclaimed Khafre, noticing that Jade was only wearing a T-shirt.

"Ummm… This is going to be very interesting," declared Jade, crossing her legs to contain the itch her Kitty was having.

"What'chu got under that shirt?"

Jade uncrossed her legs, stood pigeon-toed, and lifted her shirt, showing her perfectly-waxed pussy. For a moment, it seemed as if time had stopped. Jade's pretty, fat, and intact pussy had Khafre in a trance, until the annoying sound of a dryer going off brought him back to reality.

"I take it you like what you see," boasted Jade as she walked past Khafre to remove the clothes from the dryer. Without saying a word, Khafre removed his shirt, put his pistol on the counter, and stepped out of his designer jeans and briefs. Jade was bent over in the dryer when she felt Khafre's finger brush across her clit.

"Mmm," moaned Jade, who then bit her bottom lip and turned her head to watch Khafre out of her peripheral. Khafre then licked his fingers and proceeded to massage Jade's clit in a circular motion.

"Ssss....oooohhh!"

"You like that?"

"Fuck! Yesss!" groaned Jade.

Khafre inserted two fingers in Jade's pussy, causing her to gasp. Khafre couldn't believe the vice-like grip that Jade's walls had around his fingers. He moved his fingers in and out of her pussy at a steady pace, causing Jade to get wetter by the second.

"Oh shiiiit! Ssss…. Don't stop, daddy!" cried Jade.

Khafre could feel her juices dripping down his fingers, as her pussy to smack.

"Damn, this pussy drippin'!" Khafre snatched his fingers out of Jade's throbbing pussy.

Jade turned around and got on her knees. Khafre grabbed her by the throat with his left hand, then put his right, middle, and index fingers in her mouth, forcing her to suck the juice from his fingers, all the while moaning. He removed his fingers, then guided her mouth to his pulsating dick. Jade sucked the head of Khafre's, dick making sure to clean and swallow all pre-cum. Then, without warning, she took Khafre in her mouth whole.

"Shiiit!" moaned Khafre, grabbing the back of Jade's head.

Jade bobbed her head chaotically up and down as she moaned and sucked Khafre like a porn star. She took Khafre's dick out of her mouth, spit on it, then went back to work.

"Ooohhh…You nasty, bitch! That's it, eat that dick up," declared Khafre, knees nearly buckling.

Jade stopped momentarily, looked Khafre in his eyes, then took him in her mouth whole while massaging his balls. Khafre could feel the back of her throat. She had no gag reflex.

"Oh shit!" yelled Khafre.

When Jade snatched Khafre out of her mouth, cum shot from his dick and landed on her face. Jade ejaculated everything Khafre had in him onto her face. Jade's animalistic ways kept Khafre with a hard-on.

"Turn around," ordered Khafre.

"Yes daddy," replied Jade, doing as she was told.

"Take all dem clothes outta da dryer."

Jade snatched all the laundry from the dryer onto the floor. Khafre then forced her head into the dryer, got on his knees, and pushed down in Jade's dripping pussy from behind. Khafre and Jade moaned in unison. Khafre licked his thumb, then worked it into Jade's ass as he stroked her pussy long and deep.

"Oh, fuuccck! Ssss...yes daddy! Fuck me!" cried Jade.

Khafre now had his whole thumb in her ass. He held it there, and then picked up the pace, fucking Jade in a frenzy, causing her head to hit the back of the dryer. Jade's moans echoed inside the dryer as she came back to back, creaming all over Khafre's dick. The sounds of Jade's pussy smacking brought Khafre to a climax.

"Grrr. Shit! Ah, fuck!" yelled Khafre.

"Yesss! Nut in this pussy, daddy!" cried Jade while throwing her pussy back.

Khafre's whole body got weak, causing him to pull out of Jade and collapse on the kitchen floor.

"Damn, that pussy snatchin'," Khafre stated, out of breath.

Jade turned around and got whatever Khafre had left in him with her mouth.

"What can I say? I've been blessed," Jade retorted.

"Blessed with good pussy...yes. Cooking skills, no!" clowned Khafre, who could smell Jade' food burning.

"Dammit!" yelled Jade, rushing up to check her burning cornbread. When she pulled the pan out, her cornbread was burnt to a crisp. "Oh my God, man. I can see now, fucking with you is going to be a distraction," pronounced Jade, letting the kitchen window up to let some of the smoke out.

"From what? Harry Potter?" clowned Khafre.

"You know what? Fuck you," Jade replied, slapping Khafre's chest.

"Say no more," replied Khafre, grabbing his dick and slipping back into Jade's temple.

CHAPTER 9
DA FUCKIN' REAPER

Hezron had Amber's African style braids wrapped in his right hand and his left hand full of her left ass cheek as he power fucked her from the back.

"That's it, nigga, fuck dis pussy! Sss… Shit, yeah! Give it to me!" Amber moaned through clenched teeth.

"Damn, dis pussy, bitin'!" declared Hezron.

"Ssss….Ooohh. This pussy skeetin'!" Amber moaned, clutching the sheets.

Amber's pussy got wetter and clamped around Hezron's dick, causing him to go bananas. Hezron applied pressure, causing Amber's head to hit the headboard. Amber was on an x-pill called a monkey, so hitting her head on the headboard only turned her on more.

"Shit, I'm cummin' again, nigga. Fuck!" Out of nowhere, Amber's four-year-old Kwymaine busted through the door.

"What'chu doing to my mommy?" cried Kwymaine.

"Get'cha, li'l ass outta here, nigga!" yelled Hezron still fucking Amber from the back.

Kwymaine mean mugged Hezron, then slammed the door. He then let go of Amber's braids, grabbed both of her juicy ass cheeks, and dog fucked her until he came. When Hezron pulled out of her and laid back, Amber quickly turned around, snatched the rubber off, and sucked Hezron's dick clean.

"Animal!" yelled Hezron, grabbing Amber's head while she made his toes curl.

An hour later, Amber was still sucking Hezron's dick.

"Damn, hoe! You tryna suck da skin off a nigga dick?" Hezron pushed Amber's head away from him.

"I see you can't handle me when I get like dis," stated Amber, jaws locking from the ecstasy pill.

"Hoe, you tweakin'! I'm finna lay back and blow dis purp," replied Hezron, grabbing a blunt from the night stand and lighting it up.

"And why you kept fucking me when my son came in here? You ain't right," said Amber, lighting a cigarette. "What? I'm supposed to stop gettin' money, 'cause he brought his li'l bad ass in here? Shid…I know that ain't his first time seeing his mama in da Japanese Booty Squeeze!" exclaimed Hezron. "Boy, whatever. Anyways, wassup wit' me and you?" questioned Amber, biting her bottom lip. "Don't start that goofy shit. You know what it is. We just kicking it." "That's my dick now!" Amber declared. "Yeah, a'ight," Hezron retorted with an air of dismissal. "I'm finna go take a shower. You gon' join me?" Amber asked seductively. "Nall, I'm cool," replied Hezron. He grabbed the remote to flip through the channels.

It had been nearly an hour, and Amber was still in the shower. Hezron was about to go check on her when he heard the back door open and close. Moments later, a tall, light-skinned figure walked through the room door.

"Nigga, who the fuck is you?" asked Tremaine with a screw face.

All in one swift motion, Hezron slipped his hand from under a pillow, waving a Glock 27. He made his way around the bed all the while, still smoking his blunt.

"Um, da fuckin' reaper, nigga! Fuck wrong wit'chu creepin' in here!" Hezron pronounced, his Glock in Tremaine's neck. Tremaine held his hands in the air and fixed his eyes on the ceiling, afraid to look Hezron in his eyes.

"A'ight, my nigga. You got it," Tremaine stated, voice cracking.

"I know I got it, nigga," replied Hezron, putting his blunt out on Tremaine's cheek.

"Ahhh!" yelled Tremaine, grabbing his face.

Hezron swung his pistol and cracked Tremaine across his head, dropping him. Hezron then went to work on him.

"Get off my daddy!" yelled Kwymaine.

Amber emerged from the bathroom completely naked.

"Kwymaine, get in your room! Now!" ordered Amber. Kwymaine did as he was told. "Tremaine? What'chu doing in my fuckin' house?"

Hezron stop hitting Tremaine and just stood over him, pointing his Glock.

"I told you leave my fuckin' keys on the table. Now look at'cha dumb ass," stated Amber, going in Tremaine's pocket. She took her house key and the money he had in this pockets. Hezron kicked Tremaine in the face.

"Get'cha bitch ass outta here, nigga!" demanded Hezron.

Tremaine stumbled to his feet and headed out the same way he came in. "I'ma see you, bitch! You too, nigga!" yelled Tremaine before rushing out the back door.

 Hezron started to pursue him, but Amber stopped him.

"That's my baby daddy. He pussy! He ain't gon' do shit."

Hezron knew better though. He knew that he and Tremaine would cross paths again. That's just how the universe worked.

Amber dropped to her knees and pulled Hezron's dick out. "Let me eat that dick up."

Hezron obliged.

Khufu

Khufu

CHAPTER 10
LIGHTS OFF

Machi was in the B.G's (Bookers Garden) at Crystal's apartment, laid back on the sectional couch, blowing loud. After the incident at Arkbar's tattoo shop, Machi and Crystal kept in touch. He admired how versatile she was with her hustle. Crystal did hair, nails, sold X pills, and did fraud all in the same house. Standing 5'7" with the body of a yoga instructor, Crystal's beauty was riveting. She had long, natural black wavy hair, big light brown eyes, a round face, and flawless skin that resembled brown sugar. As gorgeous as she was, Machi decided to keep their relationship strictly platonic.

Crystal had a client by the name of Shantera who was getting her hair done when her childhood friend Tweet came through the front door.

"Heyyy boo," sang Tweet as she approached Crystal and kissed her on the cheek.

"Wassup, girl? I'm feelin' them thigh-high Balenciaga boots, bitch," pronounced Crystal.

"Yasss. Bitch, you know I gotta stay in the loop," Tweet replied, flicking her tongue out as she looked back at Machi and twerked.

"Bitch, you too much, Lock my door. I thought I had locked it."

Tweet locked Crystal's door, then headed over to the sectional couch and sat next to Machi. Tweet had the body of a stripper. Her teeth were snow white, and her skin black as tar. She had chingy eyes that made her look high all the time, but also added to her undeniable beauty.

"Boy, who are you, wit' your sexy self?" Tweet asked, rubbing her hands on Machi's thigh.

"I see you aggressive wit' it," Machi said.

"Girl, leave my friend alone, 'fore you fuck around and give him Covid or some shit, hoe!" asserted Crystal.

"Bitch, me and dis pussy is fully vaccinated," Tweet retorted, patting her pussy.

Crystal laughed. "How you know he want'chu all over him like that? Give that man some room, bitch. Social distance, hoe!"

"You mind if I sit by you, boy? What dey call you? Where you from?" questioned Tweet.

"Machi. I'm from Sunland Gardens and you straight." Machi stated, taking a pull from his blunt.

"Machi, I told you, we friends," added Crystal. "Don't pay her no mind, Machi."

"She a'ight, she's just kickin' da bo bo," said Machi.

"Yeah, I'm just kicking it!" exclaimed Tweet, rolling her neck at Crystal.

"So like I was sayin', since you ain't fuckin' Crystal you might as well climb up in dis good, wet pussy," Tweet declared, grabbing a handful of Machi's dick.

Crystal's client Shantera put her hand over her mouth, surprised at how bold Tweet was.

"Hoe, you're embarrassing me in front of my company!" pronounced Crystal. Seconds later, someone knocked on the door. "Bitch, get da door," demanded Crystal.

"Calm down, Crystal. You said, y'all ain't fuckin'. That means that dick available!" exclaimed Tweet, getting up to open the door.

"Respect my company, damn!"

Tweet opened the door and a dark-skinned male walked through the door. Crystal was suddenly nervous, but played it off.

"Hey Smoke. What'chu need?" asked Crystal.

"Let me get five red monkeys." Smoke went into his pocket, pulled out fifty dollars, and handed it to Crystal for the X pills.

Crystal went into her room to get the pills as fast as she could. Machi already recognized who Smoke was when he entered the apartment. He just didn't want to disrespect Crystal's spot. Smoke turned around and locked eyes with Machi.

"Oh, you that bitch-ass nigga from the tattoo shop," Smoke stated, reaching under his shirt.

Machi laughed in Smoke's face. "Yeah dat be me," replied Machi, calm as a lake, still smoking his blunt. "What up wit' it?"

"Nigga, you know what it is!" declared Smoke, moving around theatrically.

Machi knew that Smoke was faking. A real killer would have been upped and squeezed, especially the way Machi handled Smoke at the shop. Machi stood up and walked toward Smoke just as Crystal was coming out of her room.

"Nigga, you ain't on nothin'," Machi stated, drawing his pistol smooth as a Swiss clock and jamming it in Smoke's mouth, knocking out his two front teeth.

"Machi, no! My daughter in the room asleep. Please!" begged Crystal while Tweet looked on in admiration, pussy juices flowing.

Blood dripped from Smoke's mouth onto Machi's pistol. Smoke made sounds that resembled the words "okay man", but came out muffled.

"Next time you see me, it's lights out, nigga," assured Machi. "Turn yo' bitch ass around."

Smoke did as he was told. "Don't kill me, man!" cried Smoke.

"Machi, please," begged Crystal, who thought Machi was about to plant one in Smoke's head.

Machi grabbed the back of Smoke's shirt and wiped the blood from the gun. He then pushed Smoke into the kitchen.

"Catch you later, Crystal. Nice to meet'chu, Tweet," Machi said, and then left Crystal's apartment.

"Ooowwww, bitch! Give me his number! I gotta have that dick!" exclaimed Tweet.

Khufu

CHAPTER 11
BLOOD MONEY

Khafre hopped in his new F-350 that he had Shantel purchase for him and headed to Naples, Florida. Three and a half house later. he pulled into the Port Royal Marina, where Hanna and Samantha were waiting out front in two-piece bathing suits. There appeared to be a suave, white, red-headed male in his mid-thirties standing with the twins. When Khafre parked and hopped out of his truck, he noticed that it was a perfect day to be on the water. The sun was blazing down and the atmosphere just appeared to be placating. Khafre felt as if he was breathing air of a richer kind. He was enjoying the ambience as Hanna and Samantha made their way over.

"Heyyy, babe," Hanna greeted, hugging him and kissing his cheek.

"We missed you," Samantha added, hugging and kissing Khafre's cheek also.

"I missed you beauties too," Khafre admitted.

"Babe, this is Jarrod. He's a friend of the family, and also your first client," Hanna pronounced, smiling.

"How it goin', bro? I'm Jarrod."

"What up? I'm Khafre. Nice to meet'chu," replied Khafre, shaking Jared's hand with a firm grip. He noticed the Audemar on Jarrod's wrist.

"Pleasure to meet you too. I've heard nothing but great things."

"Is that right?" Khafre asked, checking Jarrod's apparel. Isaiah cotton shorts, Ralph Lauren loafers, and a pair of Locs sunglasses.

"Oh yeah! It's an honor, bro," Jarrod replied, removing his sunglasses to look Khafre in his eyes.

"I appreciate chu givin' me this opportunity. Let me grab my equipment before we go in." Khafre turned to grab his equipment.

"Don't worry about it, bro. I have everything you need already set up. Come on back," said Jarrod, waving for Khafre to follow him.

Khafre followed with the twins behind him. Jarrod used a key card to gain entry, letting Khafre know that anybody could not just welcome themselves in. It was strictly for the elite. Khafre followed Jarrod, stepping from a wharf onto the dock. He admired all the different boats in between each slip and noticed that the boats appeared to be larger the further you went out on the deck.

"Here we are," said Jarrod, stopping in front of Ferretti. "You want a tour?"

"Maybe afterwards. I prefer to get the job done first. Fuckin off is secondary," proclaimed Khafre, drawing a smile from Jarrod.

"Okay, bro. Whatever you want to do, man. Listen, I got a skiff down there so you can get around the yacht. I'll be on the main deck having a drink. Come find me when you're done."

"A'ight, got'chu," replied Khafre.

Jarrod boarded the yacht and disappeared.

"Listen, y'all make sho' y'all clean the inside of this yacht meticulously."

"Fuuuuuccckk that! Baby, he has a crew of like fifteen to twenty on board. They can clean up the paraphernalia of the rich. There's a hot tub on the main deck. Me and Samantha will be soaking these pink salmon. Join us when you're done," Hanna stated, rubbing her hand across her pussy.

"If he got people to clean the yacht, why the fuck he gave me the job?"

"Ask him when you're done, babe," Hanna replied, smiling as if she knew something she wasn't conveying.

"See you soon, daddy," Samantha added, grabbing Hanna by the hand and leading her on board.

"Da fuck y'all got goin' on?" Khafre asked.

Hanna blew Khafre a kiss before heading to the main deck. Khafre shook his head, made his way down to the skiff, and got to work. Three hours later, hot and jaded, Khafre boarded the yacht and found Jarrod in the cockpit smoking Parisian cigars.

"How was it?" asked Jarrod, smiling, already knowing the answer.

Khafre took a seat next to Jarrod and looked him in his eyes. "Dis my first and last time fuckin' wit' dis shit. I'ma pay somebody to do dis shit, next time," Khafre declared, drawing laughter from Jarrod.

"Now you're thinking like a boss - no disrespect intended. I know you can afford to hire someone to clean this yacht, but you had the mind to get out there and do it yourself. I admire that," Jarrod admitted.

Khafre stared at Jarrod attentively, taking in every word. Something was in the air and Khafre could feel it.

"Have a drink with me, bro," pronounced Jarrod, grabbing a bottle of Grand Vin De Chateau and pouring himself a glass.

"I'on drink wine, but, ah... What's that?" questioned Khafre, pointing at a different bottle.

"That's Japanese whiskey."

"I'll sip on that."

Jarrod poured Khafre a shot. "Cheese? Caviar?" offered Jarrod.

"I'm cool."

Jarrod raised his shot glass and Khafre followed suit.

"Salud!" exclaimed Jarrod before they knocked their drinks back.

"Damn! That's a different taste," said Khafre, pouring another shot.

"It's the good shit, bro."

"My name is Khafre."

"Khafre, I'm sorry, man. I don't mean anything by it when I call you bro. I mean, we're all brothers and sisters of the human race."

"You a'ight. We ain't gotta get all political and shit. Just call me by my name."

"Understood. Listen, Khafre, man... I like and respect how you carry yourself. I look forward to doing business with you in the near future, if you're interested. With that being said, I want to be completely honest with you," Jarrod enunciated, pouring another shot.

"What up?" Khafre asked, looking at Jarrod curiously.

"I'm pretty sure, you noticed, that my yacht was clean."

"Yeah, I peeped that. I just thought maybe... Shid, rich people keep their luxurious shit maintained," Khafre admitted.

"You're right, we do. But my reason for giving you this job was simply a way for me to get close enough to you, to propose a proposition."

"A proposition? A proposition, like what?"

"Heyyy, daddy!" yelled Hanna and Samantha in unison from the main deck.

"How, my babies doin'?" asked Khafre, smiling. "Give me a minute! I'll be up there!"

Both women giggled, then headed back to the hot tub.

"Khafre, I know what you do. These twins already let me in on it, and the teardrops in your face are definitely confirmation," voiced Jarrod.

"Man, I'on know what'chu speaking on. Cracka, you trippin'!" Khafre stated, standing to his feet.

"Okay, wait. Just calm down for a minute and let me talk to you.

"Ain't shit to talk about! You trippin', fa real!" Khafre pronounced.

Jarrod went into his wallet and removed a check. "Are you sure, there's nothing else to talk about?" Jarrod asked, pushing the check towards Khafre.

Khafre eyed Jarrod before picking the check up to examine it. The check was for one-hundred thousand dollars. Khafre glanced at Jarrod, looked at the check again, then back at Jarrod.

"Take yo' shit off," demanded Khafre.

Without argument, Jarrod removed his shirt. "I'm not a fucking, narc, okay? I'm as solid as they come," assured Jarrod.

Khafre had a seat and poured another shot. "I'm listening."

"Listen, I'll give you the address to all my homes and the schools where my daughter goes if you don't trust me. Please, man, I need you," pleaded Jarrod.

"I said I'm listening," replied Khafre, downing a shot of Japanese whiskey.

"A close associate of mine is having an affair with my wife. He's been laying up in my six-million-dollar mansion, with my wife and thinks that I'm oblivious to the fact. My wife won't let me see my kids, and she's threatening me with talks of divorce. I want you to take care of them," Jarrod said, lighting a cigar.

"Them?"

"Yeah - them. She's trying to ruin everything I've built from the ground up. I can't have that," Jarrod stated, coldly.

"And yo' kids?"

"What about them?"

"Growing up without their mother could be caustic to the mental," Khafre added.

"Cross that ocean when I get there."

Khafre nodded his head up and down before replying. "I'ma take care of dis shit, but'chu gotta do something for me."

"Name it."

"Every time I take a contract, I'll bring you the money in cash in exchange for a check, written out to my company."

"You want me to wash blood money? No problem, I got'chu, bro. I mean, Khafre."

Khafre laughed, then poured two shots to seal the deal.

"Salud!" said Jarrod.

Khufu

CHAPTER 12
YOU KNOW ME

It was five minutes after three in the morning when Khafre and Sito pulled up to their location. It was muggy, and a wall of fog obscured their view of the residents, but the GPS read 1826 7th Street, Naples, Florida.

"Tighten up. We here," Khafre muttered, tucking his FN 502 with a suppressor.

"You sho' dis it?" Sito asked, gripping his MP-5 with silencer.

"Yeah, nigga, come on," Khafre stated just above a whisper, pulling his ski mask down before exiting the stolen Benz.

As the duo tiptoed around the side of the mansion, Khafre noticed how quiet it was. No sounds of cricket or frogs. Just complete silence. The feeling was strange, but Khafre pushed on. All of a sudden, the motion lights were activated, startling Sito, causing him to pause.

"Come on," muttered Khafre slipping through a gate that the maintenance man forgot to lock.

Moments later, the motion lights cut off as Khafre and Sito rounded the massive pool and hot tub. When Khafre reached the cherry oak and glass door, he used the key that Jarrod had given him to gain entry. The pair slipped in slick as oil and slithered through the dimly-lit home with diligence. The bottom of the house was clear, so Khafre motioned for Sito to follow him up the spiral stairs that led to a spacious hallway. Khafre swung left into the first room while Sito swung right into a room a few feet away. The room Khafre entered was clear. The room Sito entered was clear also, but he pocketed the jewelry of one of Jarrod's daughters. Khafre moved toward the third room and saw that the door was cracked. When he peeked in, he saw the man that fit the description of the picture Jarrod had shown him. It was Tim, Jarrod's wife's boyfriend. He had his back towards the door, and appeared to be masturbating as he stood in front of a bed with both of Jarrod's daughters sound asleep in it. Khafre's blood boiled as he exhaled, seething, and crept in the room with gun raised.

Fop!

Khafre put one in Tim's head. The thud from his body hitting the ground caused one of Jarrod's daughters to stir, but she remained asleep. Khafre grabbed Tim by his legs and dragged him in the hallway at the same time that Sito was coming out of the room across the hall. Sito immediately went into the dead man's pockets and removed his wallet.

"Come on, bih," whispered Khafre.

Khafre and Sito checked two more rooms that were clear, then headed to the last one on the right side of the hall. When Khafre entered the room, Jarrod's wife sat at a custom-made vanity, powdering her nose with Peruvian finest. As soon as Laretta raise her face from the plate full of coke, she saw two masked men in the mirror standing behind her. Khafre had his gun raised as he spoke calmly.

"If you make a sound, I'ma kill your daughters. Understand?"

Laretta nodded her head, wiping the coke residue from her nose.

"You know why I'm here?" questioned Khafre as Sito moved closer, gun aimed at Laretta's face.

"Money?"

"Nawl." Sito glanced at Khafre with a contorted face.

"Da fuck if we ain't. Where it at?" asked Sito.

"Nigga, shut da fuck up when I'm talking," pronounced Khafre through clenched teeth.

"Who da fuck you think you talkin' to, my nigga?" implored Sito, taking his attention away from Laretta.

"Nigga, you know me," Khafre replied, smirking behind his mask.

"Nall, nigga, you know me," added Sito, taken a step towards Khafre.

Laretta turned around and diverted Sito's attention back towards her. Khafre started to hit him, but instantly thought of the times Sito saved his life.

"I'll give you the money." Laretta snatched Sito's mask off, then spit in his face before attempting to run.

Khafre grabbed Laretta by her hair, pulled her to the ground, then stuck his gun in her mouth.

"At first, I had second thoughts about killing you and taking you away from your daughters. But I see you in here caking ya li'l nose up when ya boyfriend was in your daughters' room, jacking his little dick over them as they slept peacefully. You don't deserve to live," Khafre stated, snatching his gun from her mouth and standing to his feet. He then nodded his head at Sito to handle his bidness. Khafre knew Sito didn't kill women and kids, but she left him no option. Laretta had seen his face and spit in it. Besides, Khafre wanted to see Sito put in some work. Either he killed Laretta, or Khafre would kill them both.

Sito stood over Laretta with tears streaming down his face. "Look at what da fuck you made me do," said Sito, squeezing there shots from his MP-5 into Laretta's face. Sito was so distraught about killing a woman that he no longer desired to search for anything of value. He turned to leave with Khafre right behind him, leaving Loretta and Tim to be found by her daughters.

Back in the car, there was an awkward silence, and the tension was thick in the air as Khafre drove. Sito gazed out of the window, brimming with emotion, and occasionally glancing at Khafre, then back out the window. Khafre peeped this and decided to check the temperature.

"What up, nigga, you good?" asked Khafre somewhat threateningly.

Sito turned his attention towards Khafre before speaking. "I feel some type of way, my nigga. You disrespected me in front of that bitch."

"Nall, nigga, you disrespected me when I was trying to get my point across. Da fuck you askin' for money for when I'm paying you more than enough for the job?"

"Nigga, when you home invade, robbery come wit' da territory. I'on know what kind of niggas you be doing missions wit', but all that fair game wit' me. Then, you made me kill that bitch. You know how I feel about women and kids, my nigga," pronounced Sito.

"Nigga ,we supposed to be in and out. Da fuck you wanna waste time looking for some shit that's prolly not even there for when I'm payin' you ten bands?"

Sito looked Khafre up and down intently as his pulse throbbed through his temple.

"And all that talk about women and kids shit is a dub! Nigga, she seen yo' face. You had to handle up," explained Khafre pulling into a Wal-Mart.

Sito exhaled seethingly. ,"Look my nigga, I hear what'chu saying, but you still shoulda never disrespected me in front of that bitch. You could pull my coat on that later, my nigga."

"You right, my nigga, That's my bad." Khafre was ready for the conversation to be over with. Khafre parked next to a rental car that he had Hanna rent for him.

"If you gon' fuck wit' me, fuck wit' me the right way. You supposed to be my nigga."

"I hear you, brah. Do me a favor doe."

"What's up?"

"Look in da glove box." Sito opened the glove box and saw an envelope. "It's ten bands in that envelope. That's you. Don't do no joy ridin' in dis whip. Make sho' you put dis bitch in Taylor's Creek. You hear me?"

"I got'chu, brah," Sito assured, smiling as he fanned through the money he just made. "I love you, my nigga. I fuck with'chu, for real."

Khafre glanced at Sito before getting out of the car. "That money got'chu emotional and shit. Get right, nigga," Khafre stated exiting the stolen Benz.

Sito slid in the driver's seat and poked his head out of the window. "Whatever, nigga, I love you! I'ma call you tomorrow," proclaimed Sito.

"Already," replied Khafre, getting in his rental and pulling off.

On the highway headed back to Fort Pierce, Khafre's thoughts were all over the place. He knew Sito was a killer, but he had shown a weakness, and that was bad for business. Khafre wanted to surround himself with vicious killers who had no picks. If a man, woman, or child came up on a contract, they had to be willing to execute with no hesitation. He'd made his mind up to fall back from Sito, at least on the business aspect.

Three hours later, Khafre was back in Fort Pierce. It was thirty minutes after six, and traffic was heavy with people headed to work. Khafre pulled his phone out and dialed Jade's number.

"Hello?" answered Jade.

"What good, why you up so early?"

"I'm up reading Harry Potter. What's your excuse?"

"Just got done handlin a li'l bidness. You want some company?" Khafre asked.

"What'chu gon' do to me, when you get here?" Jade asked seductively.

"I'm outside. Open the door so I can show yo' thick ass what time it is."

"It's open. Come show me."

Khufu

CHAPTER 13
LIKE FATHER, LIKE SON

Khafre laid in a lethargic type state after fucking Jade all morning. He had been trying to get a few hours of sleep, but Jade kept putting his dick in her mouth, making it nearly impossible. After sucking him dry, Jade finally let Khafre fall asleep for nearly an hour. She rubbed on Khafre's chest and watched him as he slept. When Khafre opened his eyes, he found Jade staring at him.

"What the hell is wrong wit'chu?" Khafre asked, already knowing the answer.

"Boy ain't nothing wrong with me. You are a beautiful, man. I like watching you while you sleep. Does that make you uncomfortable?" Jade smiled from ear to ear.

"That shit a li'l creepy. You wasn't doin' no Harry Potter witch craft shit over a nigga or nothing, was you?"

"You're doing the most right now."

Khafre laughed. "Come here," demanded Khafre, pulling Jade close and kissing her. "I enjoy you," Khafre admitted.

"Umm...I enjoyed you more," Jade replied, kissing Khafre again. "Who are the twins?" Jade caught Khafre off-guard.

"Damn, you went through my shit?"

"No, I wouldn't do that, but I did look at the caller ID. They were blowing your phone up."

Khafre made a mental note that Jade was possibly crazy.

"So, who are the twins?"

"Bidness partners."

"Bidness partners, huh? What kind of bidness partners?"

"I have a yacht cleaning bidness."

"Where did you meet 'em?"

"When I first got outta prison, I fucked 'em. Now we in bidness together."

"Mixing business with pleasure, I see."

"It's always a pleasure to handle my bidness, " Khafre retorted briskly.

"Okay, smart ass. It's not wise to mix the two."

"It is if you use one to facilitate the other."

"So what is this? What we doing?"

"Shid... We havin' a moment."

"And what if I'm not content with just a moment?"

"Listen. I live a nefarious life, ma. You might wanna just enjoy the moment," advised Khafre.

"All that going to prison and shit is played out. You know that, right?"

"That come wit' the life I live."

"I guess," replied Jade, rubbing on Khafre's chest. "Who are these people you got tattooed on you?"

Khafre exhaled before speaking. "My pops, my godmother, and my soulmate."

"Soulmate?"

"Leave that alone," Khafre advised.

"Understand. And the tear drops?"

"I went to the school of homicide, and graduated wit' honors. After putting in countless hours and work, I was able to get a doctorate in murda," said Khafre with casual arrogance.

"Alma mater of murder, huh?" Jade replied sardonically.

"Already."

"You too much for your damn self. But I guess." She stated, placing a kiss on Khafre's chin. She then straddled him, but his phone rang. It was the twins.

"Talk to me," answered Khafre.

"Heeeey daddy, it's me, Samantha."

"What up, ma? Where's Hanna?"

"She stepped out for a minute."

"Okay. You a'ight?"

"Yeah, I'm fine, daddy. I'm calling to let you know that we have a client lined up."

"Hire some people to handle that."

"Okay, babe. And one more thing. Jarrod wants to have a sit down this weekend."

"Say no more."

"See you there, daddy."

70

"Give Hanna my love," said Khafre as another call came in. Khafre clicked over. "What up, Unc?"

"Nephew! How you been?" asked Offtop enthusiastically.

"You already know, I'm out'chere."

"Come see me ASAP."

"Already."

***

Khafre pulled up to the Brown Store on 25th and sparked a blunt. He took a few pulls then hopped out, brushing the guts from the cigar off of his YSL sweats.

"Damn! Who I gotta kill?"

Khafre looked up and saw a gorgeous redbone. She had natural shoulder length hair, a righteous body, and multiple beauty marks on her face that rectified her beauty.

"What'chu mean, ma?" Khafre took another toke from his blunt.

"Fine as you is, I know you gotta li'l girlfriend. Point me in the right direction, so I can give her family something to do."

Khafre laughed before replying. "That was cute, I like that."

"I like you. What we gon' do 'bout that?"

"What'cha name is, miss lady?"

"Lexus. What they call you?"

"Khafre."

"Khafre who?"

"Moss."

"Khafre Moss? I know your people. You related to Baby G?"

"Yeah, that's my father. He done passed over now doe."

"Yeah, I know. I'm sorry about that. Me and your father were good friends. If you're anything like him, LAWD!" pronounced Lexus shaking her head.

"You already know I got da blood of my father," Khafre declared in a conceited tone.

"Damn, you lucky you are too young. I'll take yo li'l ass up through there!" Lexus exclaimed, rubbing on Khafre's chest and pressing her pelvis against his side. "Umm...strapped up, shorty, huh?" said Lexus after brushing against the pistol that Khafre had tucked on him.

"I keep it on me."

Lexus grabbed a handful of Khafre's dick. "Like father, like son."

"I'll give ya all da hell you lookin' for," Khafre voiced, pulling on his blunt.

"I'm on Avenue S in them purple and white apartments, apartment B. Stop by any time." Lexus walked off and got in her car.,

"Yes, suhhh," Khafre muttered to himself as he headed towards the entrance of the store.

Right when he reached for the door, it opened abruptly, and a familiar face came out. As soon as Khafre recognized who it was, he reached and upped his pistol. The familiar face was KD. KD was the same nigga who tried to rob Khafre in the bathroom at school a few years ago.

"Whoa, whoa, whoa! Chill, brah! I'on want no smoke wit'chu," KD admitted, dropping a pack of chocolate mini Dutches on the ground and raising his hands in surrender.

"You niggas told on me, nigga! I should push yo' shit back," Khafre stated through clenched teeth, holding his Glock 30 steady pointed directly in KD's face.

"On everything I love, that was them niggas I was with. I had to find out the hard way them niggas was never solid. I ain't never told on a nigga, brah."

"Nigga, fuck all that! Dem yo niggas. They sins fall on you."

"I understand that, but brah, that was years ago, and I'on even fuck wit' them niggas no more. I'on want no smoke, brah."

Khafre studied KD's face and body movements to see if he was sincere. He then lowered the pistol and tucked it, keeping a firm grip on it.

"Ain't no pressure, brah," KD proclaimed, bending down to pick up the box of Dutches, but keeping an eye on Khafre.

"You say you ain't tell on me, I respect that." Khafre puffed on his blunt, still clutching his pistol.

"So, what's been up wit'cha? I been hearing yo name, ranging out here in these streets, brah."

"Oh yeah? What dey talkin; 'bout?" questioned Khafre.

"I heard you been getting off. I'm on that same shit too now. We need to link up," KD suggested.

"Shoot me the math." KD gave Khafre his number. "I'ma have something for you real soon, brah.

"Already," KD replied.

Khufu

CHAPTER 14
AIR DIS BITCH OUT!

CC opened the door and welcomed Khafre in. As soon as Khafre crossed the threshold, a delightful smell penetrated his nose.

"Auntie, what that smell is?" Khafre asked, rubbing his stomach.

"Garlic noodles, steak, and shrimp. You want a plate?" CC asked, smiling, always happy to see her nephew.

"Yes, ma'am."

"A'ight, I'ma bring it to you. You alrighty know where your uncle at," CC stated, heading to the kitchen. Before Khafre reached the living room, he could hear the money machine beeping.

"Damn, all Unc do is count money," Khafre thought out loud entering the living room.

"Nephew!"

"Unc! What da lick read?" Khafre greeted, dabbing Offtop up.

"You see what it is. You already know the routine. Grab one of them leaves and fire up. Pour yo' drank too."

Khafre went through the familiar ritual, firing up a blunt and pouring a cup of liquor. "So how bidness going, Unc?" Khafre downed a shot of 1738 Remy.

"Bidness been proliferating, as usual. A few minuscule mishaps, but'chu know, bidness is bidness," Offtop said, loading the money machine.

"I hear that. So what's up? Why did you want me to pull up on you ASAP?" Khafre hit the blunt before passing it to Offtop.

"Remember I told you Jack put a nigga on my plug?'

"Yeah, I remember."

Offtop took a pull from the blunt before speaking. "Grab that folder off the table. I want'chu to punish this nigga," Offtop pronounced, malevolence dripping from his voice.

Khafre grabbed the folder from the table to examine its contents. After studying the photo, Khafre closed the folder and placed it back on the table. "I don't want dis one, Unc," Khafre stated pouring another shot, and taking it to head.

"I figured you were gon' say that," admitted Offtop pouring himself a shot.

Khafre looked at him perplexed. "How do you figure that?"

"I keep my eyes open, my ear to da ground, and my finger in the wind. It ain't a shit I'on know about, nephew," Offtop stated, passing Khafre back the blunt.

Khafre laid back on the couch, took a pull from the blunt, and gazed at the ceiling in deep thought.

"Here goes your plate, Khafre," said CC.

"Auntie, can you wrap it for me, please?"

"Okay, no problem, baby," CC assured, taking the plate back to the kitchen.

"We all gotta make choices in life, nephew. I just hope you make the right one with this one." Offtop downed his shot of Remy.

Khafre inhaled deeply, then exhaled, pulling out his phone. He then dialed a number that he thought he'd never call again.

"Hello?"

"Chocolate. What's up wit' it, girl?"

***

The sky was ominously dark, and the ground was dampened by a light rainfall. The streets appeared to be desolate, with the exception of stray animals. Khafre smoked a blunt as he crept down 29th Street in a stolen Crown Vic. When he got to 29th and Avenue M, he made a left and continued to creep inconspicuously. A few houses down, a male figure fell out of the yard and began to walk down the street with a panache that was familiar. Khafre pulled up on him and lowered the tinted passenger window. Startled, the man drew his pistol and pointed it in the window.

"Hold up, Sito, dis me!"

"Me who, nigga?" Sito demanded with his finger on the trigger.

"Khafre!"

"Oh, nigga...you better say something. I was finna air dis bitch out. Fuck you doin out here creepin', two in the morning?" asked Sito, tucking his pistol.

"I'm headed to the Rice Hut. Dis loud got a nigga hungry as fuck."

"Yeah, I smell it. Shid, I'm headed that way, I need some cigars. Let me ride with'cha," Sito asserted, opening the passenger's door and hopping in.

"Where are you coming from?" Khafre questioned, passing Sito the blunt.

"I'm at my bitch's house, Chocolate," replied Sito, hitting the blunt.

"Where da fuck you whip at?"

"In the shop. I'll be able to get it out next week, hopefully."

"If you need a few dollars, bitch, I gotcha."

"That's what's up. Shid… Hell yeah." Khafre crossed 25th Street and headed down Avenue M.

"I thought you were headed to the Rice Hut."

"I gotta pick dis li'l hoe up on the 23rd."

"She got a friend?" Sito asked, smiling.

"Yeah, but'cha all in love and shit. I'on wanna break up happy homes," clowned Khafre, taking it to the head.

"Man, fuck all that! Put a nigga, down."

"I gotcha, but'chu gotta tell me first."

"Tell you what, nigga?"

"You in love?"

"Nigga, you know I love that hoe Chocolate, stop playing."

"Remember I told you that hoe was poison?"

Boc!

KD put a hole in the back of Sito's head, slumping him in the front seat. Specks of blood rained on the side of Khafre's face and clothes. He used his shirt to wipe his face, reached over and grabbed the blunt that was clamped between Sito's fingers, and continued to smoke it.

"Thought you weren't gonna never give me the signal," KD stated.

"I semi-fucked wit' da nigga. It was only right that I smoked one wit 'em first."

"I hear that."

"Damn, look like dem crackas behind us," alerted Khafre.

KD turned around to see if Khafre's assumptions were correct.

Boc!

Khafre put a hole in the side of KD's head, killing him instantly. He had told KD if he wanted to be a part of what he was building, he had to put it in work. Killing Sito was the initiation, but Khafre still had ill feelings about the incident in school. Even though KD wasn't the one who was told, he was guilty by affiliation. He had to die.

Khafre pulled in the back of a beer hut on 13th Street, which was enemy turf. Sito and KD's blood had started to exude a distinctive stench that resemble salty, wet pennies. After looking around, Khafre got out and pulled both bodies out of the car, laying them side by side. He then got back in the stolen Crown Vic and pulled off. When the bodies would be discovered on the enemy's turf, the whole city would think that 13th Street Gangstaz were responsible.

Khafre pulled behind Francis K. Sweet, a school on 13th, and dumped the Crown Vic in Taylor's Creek. He then walked along the Canal Bank all the way to 25th Street and went to his apartment on top of the Brown Store. Everything had gone as Smooth as a chinchilla. He'd gotten away unscathed with another contract under his belt.

CHAPTER 15
HAPPY BIRTHDAY, NIGGA!

Khafre was sitting in his living room, smoking a blunt, scrolling down Facebook, when there was a knock at the door. Not expecting company, he grabbed his camouflage Nighthawk 10MM, and peeped through the side of his designer drapes.

"Da fuck?" Khafre muttered as he headed to the door and opened it.

"What up fam?" greeted Hezron, dapping Khafre up and entering the apartment.

"What up, Cuz?" greeted Machi.

"What's happenin'?" Khafre replied, dapping Machi up and closing the door behind him. "How da fuck y'all know where I live?" questioned Khafre, heading to the kitchen

"We went by yo' momma's house. She told us where you stay," proclaimed Machi.

"Nigga, yo' car parked outside," Hezron stated, laughing.

"I'ma have to straighten her out 'bout that."

"Nigga, we family!" pronounced Hezron, taking a seat at the counter.

"That's beside the point."

"Yeah, you trippin', fam," Machi added, having a seat in the living room.

"Y'all want something to drink?"

"I'm cool," Machi replied.

"Where da weed at?" asked Hezron.

"Open that cigar box on da table."

Machi opened the box and saw that it was filled with pre-rolled blunts. He lit one, took it to Hezron, then sat back on the couch and lit another one.

"So, what blew y'all dis way?" Khafre was still scrolling down Facebook while smoking a blunt.

"Shid… You been ghost for a few days. We just checking on ya," Hezron stated.

"I just been moving around, puttin' shit together. Aye! Aye, y'all check dis shit out!" Khafre insisted with a devilish grin. Machi and Hezron made their way over to Khafre.

"What up?" asked Hezron.

"Look, dis that nigga Smoke from the tattoo shop. Today that nigga birthday."

"I ran into that nigga a few days ago," added Machi, grabbing the phone. "I jammed my pistol in that nigga's mouth and knocked his teeth out and shit. He was as good as dead, but Crystal was crying and begging me not to kill da nigga. We was in her house and shit so I spared 'em."

"You fuckin' Crystal?" questioned Khafre.

"Nall, we just be, kicking it."

"Let me see da phone," said Hezron, grabbing the phone from Machi.

"Ain't dis some shit?"

"Wassup?" asked Khafre.

"That's da nigga Tremaine in da picture wit 'em!"

"Who da fuck is Tremaine?" Khafre asked.

"I was fuckin' da hoe Amber the other day, and dis nigga crept in through da back door and shit. I ain't know, it was da hoe's baby daddy, so I upped on that nigga's ass. Da hoe Amber come out da bathroom, seen me pistol whippin' da nigga, and went in his pockets," Hezron stated, laughing.

"That hoe on some other shit," pronounced Khafre.

"I know," Hezron added. "But anyways, da nigga was talking crazy before he left and shit. I was finna go hit da nigga, but Amber stopped me, like he just rappin'."

"Shid, it look like dem niggas posted up at dem apartments behind the Blue Store."

"What'chu niggas wanna do?" Khafre asked, putting the roach out in the ashtray.

"Smack a nigga on his birthday? Um, on that!" assured Hezron.

"It's whatever," said Machi.

"Say none," Khafre replied, grabbing his phone and dialing a number.

"Hello?"

"Jade, what's good wit' it?"

"Nothing, just laying here, thinking of you actually."

"That's good, that's what I love to hear."

"Well, it's the truth," she replied.

"Listen, let me ask you something."

"Anything."

"Would you ride for me?"

***

It was thirty minutes after twelve, and the sun was blazing down from its highest point in the cloudless sky. The traffic was mild as Jade crept down Avenue Q and made a right on 13th Street in a 2000 F-150.

She turned the radio up as Meagan Thee Stallion's "Thot Shit" blared from the speakers, and she twerked as she drove. When she got to 13th and Avenue K, she made a right and pulled on the side of the Blue Store, only allowing the front of the truck to be seen by the crowd at the apartment. Jade hopped out with a wig and sunglasses on and began to twerk with her hands on her knees. She stuck her tongue out and looked back at the crowd as she twerked both cheeks simultaneously, then in tandem, causing hysteria amongst the Young Killaz. Right when they started approaching, Jade hopped back in the truck, pulled up in front of the apartments, stopped and blew the horn. Hezron and Machi, who were laying in the bed of the truck, rose, both brandishing two pistols.

"Happy birthday, homeboy!" yelled Machi, spotting and dropping Smoke, who was closest to the truck. Tremaine's eyes widened when he saw Hezron, and he attempted to turn and run.

"Come here, boy!"

Boc!

Boc!

Boc!

Boc!

Khufu

Hezron packed Tremaine's back full of Honey Badger rounds, dropping him. Smoke's hittas reached for their weapons, but Khafre stepping out of the passenger side and rounding the truck with a Romanian AK caused hesitation, which proved to be fatal.
KAK!KAK!KAK!KAK!KAK!
KAK!KAK!KAK!KAK!KAK!
Some managed to make it around the apartments, but most were laid out on the pavement. Hezron hopped off the truck and stood over Tremaine.

"You chose da wrong hoe to have yo' baby."
Hezron put two slugs in Tremaine's skull.
"What I told you, nigga?" Machi implored, planting one in Smoke's head.

Khafre walked up and stood over a beautiful young lady named KeKe, who was sprawled out on the pavement. Khafre noted that her leg was twisted like a pretzel and laid by her head.

"Damn, dis K got dis bitch twisted out here," Khafre mutters to himself. He lifted the back of the AK and pointed the front of it down towards her face.

"Please! Please… Mann!" KeKe cried with a heavy lisp as blood poured from her nearly-decapitated limb.

Khafre decided to spare her. He then turned the AK towards the apartments and peppered them with 7.62 rounds.

"Let's slide, brah!" yelled Hezron.

Khafre hopped back in the truck and Jade pulled off. When the smoke cleared, Lotto, who was Smoke's big homie, came outside and found his li'l homies dead on the pavement and his sister on the ground bleeding dreadfully.

CHAPTER 16
YOU REACH YOU DIE

"Damn, this shit feels good," Khafre stated, making his way into the hot tub with the twins.

"Better than me?" asked Hanna straddling Khafre and placing him inside her.

"Shiiiit!" moaned Khafre, gripping Hanna's delicate ass cheeks and slowly moving her up and down on his shaft.

"Fucckkk! I've missed you, daddy," Hanna said as she gripped the edge of the hot tub.

Khafre put Hanna's left nipple in his mouth and sucked it tenderly, causing her to bounce more rapidly and cum instantly. Khafre was on the verge of cumming, but Samantha snatched Hanna off of Khafre dick and quickly placed it inside of her.

"Hey! Okay, that's enough of that shit! You ladies give me and Khafre here a moment to talk. Go tell the chef to make you something," Jarrod insisted, stepping in the hot tub.

"Way to ruin my fucking moment!" barked Samantha, rising from Khafre's lap and climbing out of the hot tub with Hanna right behind her.

"Later for you, daddy," Samantha pronounced seductively.

"You know it," replied Khafre.

"I see you gotta thing for them snow bunnies, man," noted Jarrod, smiling

"I love all women."

"Ditto! I'm wit'chu, man.

"What up, J? What'chu wanna rap about?"

"Okay, first off, I appreciate you eradicating that dilemma. It means everything to me to have my daughters."

"It was my pleasure. I enjoyed it," Khafre admitted.

Jarrod gave Khafre an evaluative look before responding. "I see you're good at what you do. I have another proposal, if you are interested. I'm taking a trip to the Bahamas next week. I need to pick something up and I wanna make sure everything goes smoothly."

"Yeah, I got'cha," said Khafre.

"There's something else."

"What up?"

"When we get halfway back, I'ma need you to bring something to shore for me.

"As long as that check cut, I ain't doing no trippin'."

"You're gonna need two more people you can trust," Jarrod assured.

"No problem."

"Okay, it's settled then. Meet me at the Marina in Fort Pierce, on Saturday. 12:30 p.m."

"I'ma be there."

"And Khafre?"

"Yeah?"

"Bring some girls along. It'll keep the suspicion down."

"Already!"

***

It was a beautiful, vibrant day, to navigate the waters of the Atlantic on a one-hundred-foot yacht. The sun was out, champagne and food were plentiful, and the women were wearing next to nothing.

"Why da fuck you putting champagne in yo' purse when the shit free?" Hezron asked Amber in disgust. "Hoe, take that shit out'cha purse, 'fore I slap yo' dumb ass with dis pistol! Damn! A nigga can't take yo' ratchet ass nowhere!"

"You ain't gotta talk to a bitch like that, Hezron. That shit free," Amber retorted, lighting a cigarette.

"You embarrassing a nigga wit' that fuck shit!"

"You call yourself checkin' me but some shit dis white man don't care about? I see yo' pettiness runs deep."

"Keep talking, hoe. I'ma throw yo' ass overboard," threatened Hezron, drawing laughter from Machi, who was sitting across from him on an overstuffed sofa between Crystal and Tweet.

Amber exhaled and continued to smoke her cigarette in silence.

"Thank you for inviting me out here, Machi. This shit is so beautiful and relaxing. I needed this!" exclaimed Crystal, taking a sip from her champagne glass.

"Don't trip, ma. You deserve it," Machi stated, tapping Crystal on her thick blemish free thighs.

"Yeah, Machi, thank you, baby," added Tweet, rubbing her hand over Machi's chiseled chest.

"You good, Tweet," said Machi.

"Damn, hoe! Can I get a minute wit my friend without you sexually assaulting him? Damn!" expressed Crystal, face tightening with emotion.

"He is my friend too, hoe! Why you think he invited me too?"

"I invited yo' thirsty ass, not Machi," Crystal replied seethingly.

"Um… Let me find out you let a shot of dick come between us!"

Crystal waved her hand at Tweet dismissively. "I hate to see how you gonna act when I really do put dis pussy on 'em," Tweet proclaimed, smiling.

"I can't right now wit'chu! Hoe, you trippin'," Crystal stated, getting up and heading to the side of the yacht.

Machi got up and followed behind her.

"Let her go! Stay here wit' me, daddy!" pronounced Tweet.

But her wishes went unanswered. When Machi caught up to Crystal, she was leaning on the rail, gazing out at the unpredictable ocean.

"You okay?"

"Yeah, I'm alright. She is just too much for me at times."

"Come on, Crystal. You know Tweet gon' be Tweet." Machi rubbed Crystal's back gently. Crystal exhaled before replying.

"I know. She just gets on my nerves sometimes," declared Crystal, grabbing Machi's arm and wrapping it around her waist.

Machi stepped closer and wrapped his other arm around her. "What are we doing?" questioned Machi.

"Nothing. Ain't nothing wrong wit' friends holding each other."

"A'ight, ma." Machi took in the scent of Crystal's flesh as he closed in the space between them.

"Uh-uhhh! What is that I feel back there?" Crystal implored playfully, moving her thick soft ass from side to side against Machi's dick.

"Some shit you don't wanna get involved with'"

"Maybe I do."

"Let's just keep it how we got it."

"I'm cool wit' that - for now."

Machi laughed and kissed Crystal on the cheek.

Meanwhile, Khafre was in the hot tub enjoying Jade's company when Hanna and Samantha approached and asked to join them.

"Yeah, it's cool. Y'all come on in," Khafre stated.

Hanna and Samantha entered the hot tub completely nude and placed kisses on Khafre's cheek.

"Who is this, daddy?" Samantha questioned, admiring the woman's beauty.

"This is Jade," said Khafre.

"Hi," the twins replied in unison.

"She's fascinatingly gorgeous," said Hanna

"Thank you," Jade replied.

"Y'all take care of her for me."

"Sure thing, daddy," Hanna assured as she and Samantha engaged on Jade from both sides.

"Take care of me how?" Jade asked, confused.

"Relax." Hanna started placing a tender kiss on Jade's lips. Samantha placed kisses on Jade's shoulder and up her neck while slipping her hand past her bikini and stimulating her clit.

"Sss...ahhh!" moaned Jade.

"That's right, get her," taunted Khafre.

Hanna lifted Jade and placed her on the side of the hot tub and removed her bikini top and bottom. Samantha placed gentle kisses on Jade's breasts, then began to suck them gracefully, while Hanna placed kisses in between her thighs.

"Ahhh! Sss...yes!" cried Jade blissfully.

Hanna kissed Jade's clit, flicked her tongue repeatedly, then French kissed her clit.

"Yeah… Eat dis pussy!"

Samantha continued to suck Jade's titties, occasionally coming up to kiss her on the mouth. Khafre approached Hanna from behind and pushed down in her with ease.

"Mmm," Hanna moaned, still sucking on Jade's clit.

Samantha made her way around to Khafre and kissed him softly on his back as he stroked Hanna slow and steady.

"That's a good girl, suck that pussy," Khafre cheered Hanna on.

"Ohhh my Gawd!" yelled Jade, cumming for the third time while grabbing her breasts and pinching her nipples.

Hanna came right behind Jade, her walls clutching around Khafre shaft.

"Fuccck!" moaned Khafre. He kissed Samantha passionately while still stroking Hanna. When Khafre felt his nut coming, he grabbed Samantha by the hair, stood up, and shoved his dick in her mouth. The very sight of Khafre's dominance caused Jade to cum again. Samantha was able to get him rock hard again. Khafre snatched out of Samantha's mouth, moved Hanna to the side and pushed down in Jade.

"Fuck me, please!" cried Jade, wrapping her arms around Khafre's neck.

Khafre lifted Jade off the edge of the hot tub and bounced her up and down on his dick.

"Ohhh! I'm fuckin' nuttin', nigga, fuck!" Jade's pussy started to make smacking noises with every stroke, exciting Khafre and prompting him to skeet prematurely.

After planting his seeds in Jade, Khafre sat down and placed kisses on her cheeks and lips.

"You enjoyed that?" Khafre questioned, out of breath.

"I fucking loved it!" Jade admitted.

"Well, stick around for a while. These the only type of moments I'm on."

"Heyyy! No fair, daddy. You didn't give me any dick," whined Samantha.

"How do you want it?" Khafre asked, approaching Samantha and placing his hand around her throat. Before things could go any further, Jarrod approached the scene.

"What up, J?" Khafre asked, removing his hands from around Samantha's throat.

"Let me have a word with you."

"Y'all, hold it down for daddy. I'll be right back," Khafre stated, stepping out of the hot tub.

As soon as Khafre took a walk with Jarrod, Hanna and Samantha proceeded to ravish Jade again.

"You enjoying yourself?" asked Jarrod.

"Rhetorical questions?"

Jarrod laughed before replying. "You right. It's obvious that you're having a great time. But I need you to get serious. See that fishing boat approaching a few yards out?"

"Yeah," Khafre replied briskly.

"Those are our guys. Get your men on post. This should be quick."

"I'm on it," Khafre assured, then walked off.

He rounded up all the women and took them to the dining area, where the chef had prepared a full course meal. Khafre then handed Hezron a German P-40 machine gun. Jarrod used a pair of Staver 8x21 compact binoculars to see how many men the fishing boat contained. He looked at Khafre and held up three fingers. He then radioed for his captain to slow down. Five minutes later, as Jarrod's yacht slowly drifted towards the anchored fishing boat, an associate of his of European descent could be seen in the front of the boat. He had two Bahamians with him. Jarrod had met Phil during a trip to the Bahama three years ago. They'd been doing business ever since.

"Jarrod! What's with the armed men? You don't trust me, now? Come on, man," Phil stated.

"Precautionary, Phil! Besides, your men are armed too," Jarrod replied, noticing the pea shooters that the Bahamians had on their waists.

"You reach, you die!" Khafre yelled from the top deck.

"Jesus, Jarrod!" yelled Phil.

"Just throw them over, quickly!" advised Jarrod.

Phil nodded his head and one of his men quickly threw three life jackets onto the yacht. Jarrod threw a bag over to the fishing boat, then radioed for his caption to head back to Fort Pierce. "I'll call you later, Phil. Pleasure doing business with you," pronounced Jarrod, smiling.

It was a little after seven p.m. when Jarrod ordered his captain to stop the yacht. He then led Khafre, Hezron, and Machi to the back of the yacht.

"Listen. We're thirty minutes out. I want each of you to strap on a life jacket, get on these jet skis, and take them to shore. Once you make it to shore, don't worry about the jet skis. I'll take care of them. In the parking lot, you'll see a black Tahoe. The keys are under the seat. Load the life jackets in the trunk and put the keys back under the seat. Meet me at the Red Roof Inn tomorrow at twelve o'clock p.m. I'll make sure the girls get home safe."

"And what if we don't make it?" questioned Khafre.

"I have the best lawyers in the U.S.," Jarrod assured him.

"Say no more. We on it!" Khafre stated.

Khufu

CHAPTER 17
THEY GON' HIDE YOU

It was ten after twelve when Jarrod pulled into the Red Roof Inn in a Jaguar with the Tahoe trailing behind him. He quickly found a parking spot and hopped out with a duffle bag in hand. Spotting Khafre's F-350, he motioned for Khafre to follow him to the room. Khafre exited the truck and followed Jarrod to room 23. Upon entering the room, Jarrod set the duffle on the bed, then shook hands with Khafre, who then took a seat at the table by the window.

"How are you doing, man?" Jarrod asked in a congenial tone.

"All good. How 'bout yaself? How are your daughters doin'?"

"Everything's propitious, thanks to you."

"Already. So what was that in the Tahoe behind you?"

"My driver," Jarrod replied, smoothly unzipping the duffle bag and removing a life jacket. He then took a switchblade, cut the jacket open, and removed a brick of fentanyl

"Coke?"

"Fentanyl," Jarrod corrected.

"Neva, heard of it," Khafre admitted.

"Four times more potent than heroin. Thirty-six ounces, at twenty-eight hundred a piece. You can put a three on one, and get yourself four bricks if you cut with a quinine."

"Damn! Twenty-eight hunnid an ounce? That's over a hunnid bands," Khafre replied excitedly.

"Yeah, but if you get caught with this shit, they are gonna hide you. I mean for a long time"

"No risk, no glory," replied Khafre audaciously.

"I agree. Listen, if you want, I'ma give you and your men two bricks apiece for bringing them to shore."

"We call that," Khafre asserted briskly.

"Alright then," pronounced Jarrod, removing a check from his wallet. "This is sixty-thousand. That's twenty apiece for you and your men. I'll call you if I need you."

"Already."

"Khafre?"

Khufu

"Yeah?"

"If anybody dies from this shit, and it's linked to you, through an informant or your number found in the deceased person's phone, they're charging you with the body."

"Noted," Khafre replied, unbothered.

***

The next day, Khafre invited Hezron and Machi over to his apartment above the Brown Store. He gave them twenty-thousand a piece in cash and kept the check that Jarrod had made out to his yacht cleaning business. After expressing their gratitude, they all sparked a blunt while Khafre educated them on fentanyl.

"So, what's up wit' it? Y'all wit' a nigga, or what?" asked Khafre.

"Look, fam, we ain't neva really fucked wit' no shit like that," Machi stated.

"Then you talkin' 'bout all this time if we get caught, and bitches dying from this hit. Give us a few days, fam. We'll have an answer for you then," added Hezron.

"Ain't no rush. I'ma just sit on dis shit till y'all make up y'all minds. If y'all don't get back at me in two weeks, I'ma move wit'out cha!" exclaimed Khafre.

"Fair enough," Hezron replied, standing to dap Khafre up before leaving.

Machi followed suit and left behind Hezron. After locking the door, Khafre picked his phone up off the table and dialed out. The phone rang three times before a voice answered, dripping with seduction and experience

"Yesss. This is Lexus speaking."

"How you doin, miss lady?"

"Who's speaking?"

"Khafre."

"Hmm! I was wondering when you was gon' call. Wassup?"

"I'ma finna go kick it somewhere, prolly the mall or some shit. You wanna come with me?"

"Boy, I ain't got no money for that."

"Don't ever disrespect me like that again. If I'm inviting you, that means it's on me," Khafre stated.

"Well, excuse me! It's all on you, huh?"

"You heard me."

"Well, give me like fifteen minutes to wash this li'l pretty pussy."

"Don't worry about that either," Khafre replied smoothly.

"And why is that?" Lexus asked, her interest piqued.

"Cuz I'ma give you a tongue bath."

"Mmm! Boy, you just made this lil coochie jump. Hurry up and come get me."

Khafre laughed before replying. "I'm on da way."

Khafre got dipped in a Ferragamo sweatsuit, grabbed his Mossberg 9mm Luger, then jumped in his whip. When Khafre pulled in front of Lexus's apartment on Ave S, she was already standing outside looking breathtaking in a pair of low-cut denim jeans and a Hollister top that displayed her flat stomach and beautiful red skin. Her natural long hair was pulled tight into a ponytail and her accessories complemented her outfit. Khafra let down his window and blew the horn. Lexus approached the car and got in.

"You lookin' good, ma," complimented Khafre.

"You look good enough to eat yourself," Lexus replied.

"Oh yeah? I can help you facilitate that later."

Khafre headed to Jensen Beach Mall. The ride to the mall was riveting. Khafre found Lexus's personality intriguing and attractive. During the ride to the mall, there was never a dull moment. Once in the mall, Khafre spared no expense. He purchased a Givenchy minidress for $2299 and a pair of studded, fringed stilettos by Givenchy for $1995. When he offered to buy more, Lexus thanked him and refused.

While walking in the mall, engaged in an invigorating conversation, Khafre noticed two women approaching with one in a wheelchair. Once ten feet away, the woman in the wheelchair looked up, locked eyes with Khafre, and went into pure shock. Her eyes grew as she forced her wheelchair to stop abruptly and go in the opposite direction, leaving her handler.

"What's wrong with you?" asked Tiny, the friend of the girl in the wheelchair.

The girl in the wheelchair ignored her and kept looking back to see if Khafre was advancing on her.

"You know her?" questioned Lexus, her brows creased with curiosity.

"Nall, li'l mama trippin'," replied Khafre dismissively.

"Damn, she act like you put her ass in that wheelchair."

"I'on know what that be about," lied Khafre. "Let's roll out, though."

Little did Lexus know how correct she was. The woman in the wheelchair was Lotto's sister KeKe.

CHAPTER 18
JUST PULL OVER

Back in Fort Pierce, Khafre was creeping down 23rd when a police cruiser jumped behind him with the lights on.

"Damn, dem crackas behind us," informed Khafre, creeping across 23rd and Avenue E.

"Just pull over. You got a license, don't chu?" asked Lexus.

"Nawl, and I'm dirty," Khafre replied, pulling over in front of a house he was familiar with. "You know what to do," Khafre stated as he jumped out of the driver's seat and took off running.

"Don't chu fucking move!" yelled the female officer to Lexus, then took off behind Khafre.

Lexus switched over to the driver's seat and pulled off.

Once Khafre rounded the house, he snatched out his pistol and fired two shots in the air, causing the officer to pull back and draw her weapon. Khafre leaped over a fence and ran across a field that was behind it. When he came to the end of the field, Lexus pulled up in front of him. Khafre hopped in and they pulled off.

***

Lexus entered her apartment with Khafre right behind her. Khafre locked the door behind him while Lexus set her key on a coffee table. When Lexus turned around, Khafre grabbed her around the neck and stared deep into her titillating eyes. Lexus inhaled brusquely, startled with excitement. Not fully understanding what was taking place, she attempted to question Khafre's actions, but he vetoed that by pressing his lips against her. Lexus obliged as Khafre kissed her deeply, stirring a torrid storm between her legs.

"Mmm," moaned Lexus, prompting Khafre to rip the Hollister top from her flesh.

The sight of her pretty red perky titties caused Khafre's mouth to water. He placed her left nipple in his mouth while unfastening her jeans and pulling them off. Khafre pushed Lexus on the sofa and attempted to advance on her, but she stopped him, placing her hands on his six pack. She rubbed her hands over the lumps on his stomach, then grabbed his dick and sucked the head of it while caressing his balls.

"Sss...fuck!" Khafre moaned, grabbing Lexus by her ponytail.

"Nall, don't grab my hair, nigga! Put'cha hands behind your back," Lexus instructed. Khafre complied. Lexus then grabbed Khafre's dick with both hands, ran her tongue down the side of it, then took him in her mouth whole.

"Aaah! Shiiit!" Khafre whimpered, knees nearly buckling.

Lexus took Khafre's full length in and out of her mouth repeatedly as she sucked him altruistically.

"Sss...oooowww, you eating that dick up!" cried Khafre.

As soon as Khafre was about to cum, Lexus snatched him out of her mouth and blew in his pee hole gently and down his shaft. Khafre's dick pulsated with anticipation as Lexus slapped his dick in her face. She then stood, pushed Khafre down on the sofa, and straddled him, easing down on him.

"Sss...mmm!" moaned Lexus, putting her hands behind Khafre's head and gripping the couch.

Khafre gripped both of her ass cheeks, then rubbed his hands up the deep arch in her back as she rocked back and forth on him like a pendulum.

"That's it, ride this dick!" Khafre enthused.

Lexus leaned forward and licked and sucked on Khafre's ear as she picked her pace up.

"Ahhh! Oooooh!" Lexus yelled in pure bliss.

Khafre gripped her ass and began to forcefully bounce her up and down in a tortuous manner.

"Fuck! This pussy bitin'," moaned Khafre.

Lexus lifted her head to the sky, eyes rolling to the back of head.

"Shit, I'm cumming on this dick!" yelled Lexus as a torrent of juices cascaded from her body, soaking Khafre. Lexus lifted her head to the sky, eyes rolling to the back of her head. She squeezed her walls around Khafre's shaft and rotated her hips slowly as she released everything in her.

Khafre suddenly lifted her off of him and bent her over the edge of the couch.

"What'chu doin' to me?" questioned Lexus.

"Shut da fuck up!" ordered Khafre, pushing down in her from behind. Lexus yelled as Khafre smacked her ass and punished her from behind.

"Bitch! Didn't I say shut da fuck up!" Smack!

"Ooohhh, shit, daddy, I'm sorry! Please don't stop!"

Khafre grabbed Lexus by her ponytail with his right hand, yanked her head back, and gripped her left ass cheek with his left hand and rode her like a mustang.

"What they call me?" Smack!

"Shiiit! Khafre!"

"What'chu call me?" Smack!

"Sss… Daddy!"

"What da fuck my name is?" Smack!

"Ahhhh…Khafre!" Lexus cried, cumming for the third time. "Fuck! Cum in me! I want'chu to cum in me, daddy!"

Khafre let Lexus's hair go, snatched out of her, and skeeted between her cheeks.

"Aaaahhhh…Fuck!" yelled Khafre, then collapsed down on the couch.

After catching her breath, Lexus got up and headed to the bathroom to clean up. Khafre laid back in a state of bliss and thought to himself, *Damn that pussy was good.* A few minutes later, Lexus emerged from the bathroom with a wet rag and cleaned Khafre up.

"You a'ight?" asked Khafre.

"Oh, I'm all the way good."

"That's what I love to hear."

Lexus locked eyes with Khafre for a moment before speaking. "You was beating that pussy though. The right way!" Lexus admitted

"Ain't no other way. I ain't come here to play wit'chu," Khafre assured with an air of assertiveness.

"Why you ain't cum in me?"

"You say you used to fuck wit' my pops, right?"

"We just used to kick it. You know he was just a real nigga that I loved to be around, but we never fucked," lied Lexus, throwing the rag on the table and laying back on Khafre.

"I hear you."

"I'm for real."

"I said, I hear you. Look, I appreciate what'chu did today. You a solid one, for real."

"No problem. I mean, it didn't make sense to just sit in the car when I knew you needed help. Plus, the bitch didn't even have back up, so I just took off."

"I can fuck wit' somebody like you."

"What'chu mean?"

"What'chu know 'bout fentanyl?"

"I'on know too much about it, but I got a homeboy who do."

"See what type of time he on," Khafre stated.

Lexus grabbed her phone off the table and dialed out on speaker phone.

"Get at me, baby," said the voice on the phone.

"Cowboy?"

"Yeah, talk to me. Wassup?"

"This Lexus. Listen, you still fucking off?"

"Which hoe you speaking on?"

"That hoe fent."

"Of course. What about her?"

"My friend got a badder bitch then her," assured Lexus.

"Bring her here, let me look at her. If she is as bad as you say she is, I'ma fuck her."

"We'll be down there in a few hours."

"You know where I'm at. Get at me!" exclaimed Cowboy.

"Okay." Lexus ended the call.

"What'chu mean a few hours?" questioned Khafre.

"Oh, he's from Seffner, Florida."

"Da fuck is that?"

"A country-ass town, outside of Tampa."

"You trust this nigga?"

"I mean, it's been awhile since I seen him, but I know he be grabbing shit in bulk"

"A'ight, fuck it, let's go." Khafre got up to get dressed when his phone rang. "Yeah!"

"Come see me when you get a chance," said Offtop.

"A'ight, Unc. I'll be there tomorrow."

"Already!"

Khufu

CHAPTER 19
THE WHOLE THANG

It was a quarter after seven when Khafre got off of I-10 on exit 10 and entered Seffner. Lexus navigated him to Pine Street and MLK when they came across a plot of land occupied by a double wide trailer and LC 500 Coupe.

"Pull in right there," Lexus instructed.

"Damn, this shit country as fuck," stated Khafre parking behind the Lexus.

"Yeah, I know, right? But it's a lot of money out here," Lexus replied, grabbing her phone to call Cowboy.

"Get at me!"

"We are here."

"Outside?"

"Yeah."

"Come in."

"Okay." Lexus hung up the phone. "He says, come in."

Khafre grabbed his see-through Louis briefcase and attempted to open the car door, but Lexus stopped him. "What up?" asked Khafre, gazing at Lexus questioningly.

"Be careful, please," retorted Lexus, eyeing Khafre intently.

"Oh, you love me already, huh?"

Lexus smiled. "Boy, bye. I just want'chu to stay on point."

"Don't trip. I'm off safety with it," Khafre assured, exiting the car.

When he approached the door, Cowboy was standing behind the screen door. "Come on in," invited Cowboy, opening the door for Khafre.

"Go ahead, I'm right behind you," Khafre stated, not wanting Cowboy behind him.

"Okay, no problem," Cowboy replied, walking deeper into the living room.

When Khafre entered the trailer, he observed a young'un moving flaky and abnormally. He tried desperately to straighten up his posture, which Khafre found comical.

"You alright over there, li'l homie?" Khafre asked, setting his briefcase down on a small table in the living room. The young'un nodded his head in silence. "You look a li'l tense over there. You might wanna loosen up a lil bit," Khafre advised.

"Hey, hey, focus on me. He ain't on nothing," Cowboy proclaimed.

Khafre looked at the young'un, then back at Cowboy contemptuously.

"Let's see it. Where it at?"

"Where that money at, nigga?"

"You ain't even show me how much you brought. Where dey do that?" questioned Cowboy.

"I got the whole thing, nigga! Now where that paper at?"

"Brah, just open the briefcase and let me look at it. I got the paper. I'on play games like that."

Khafre opened the case and stepped back to let Cowboy examine the work. Khafre observed the young'un reaching in his pocket and reacted. He pulled his SIG Glock .357 upped and squeezed off three shots, dropping the young'un. Cowboy tucked his head and squatted low to the floor, thinking he was hit. Khafre grabbed Cowboy by his dreads and forced him over to where the young'un was laying with one hand over the hole in his neck, and the other clutching a phone.

"What the fuck, man? Fuck you shoot 'em for?"

"He reached, I had to teach 'em," Khafre stated with no compassion.

"He had a fuckin' phone, man."

"Maannn. Fuck all that! That brick going for ninety! Now, show me that paper, or I'ma leave ya ass right beside him."

"Calm down. It's in the kitchen cabinet."

"Get it, nigga!" ordered Khafre, pushing Cowboy towards the kitchen with his Glock aimed at the back of his head.

"I'm reaching for it. Don't shoot," Cowboy replied, moving cautiously. He opened the cabinet, grabbed a Wal-Mart bag, and set it on the counter. "Look, don't worry about li'l homie. I'll take care of the body," Cowboy assured with his hands raised in the air.

Khafre grabbed the bag, took a quick glance inside, then tucked it in his briefs. "Grab a knife outta the drawer."

"For what?" Cowboy retorted, perplexed.

"Nigga, grab a fuckin' knife," Khafre replied through clenched teeth. Cowboy did as he was told. "Now stab that nigga in his chest." Cowboy started to protest, but decided against it. He kneeled down and plunged the knife in the young'un's sternum.

"It was a pleasure doing bidness wit'cha, country-ass nigga," Khafre stated, backing up to the front door and making his exit. When Khafre got to the car, Lexus was already in the driver seat, so he got in on the passenger side.

"What happened? I heard gunshots."

"We good. I'on think he's gon' wanna do bidness against though," stated Khafre, smiling.

Khufu

CHAPTER 20
YOU GONNA LEARN TONIGHT

Shantell was lying comfortably on the butter soft sofa watching an episode of *Sisters* when there was a knock at the door.

"Coming!" yelled Shantell. She opened the door and was surprised at the visitor she had. "Shameeka?"

"Heyyy, Shantell, long time, no see."

"I know, right? What brings you this way?"

"Is Khafre in there?"

"No, why?"

"I hate to bring this to you, but I know you are the only one who can convince him."

"To do what?" asked Shantell, placing her hands on her hips.

"Turn himself in."

"For what? He kill somebody?" Shantell asked as her heart began to accelerate.

"No, nothing like that. Three weeks ago, I pulled him over and he got out and fled on foot. I pursued him. Right when he was rounding a house, I recognized him. Then I heard three shots, so I stopped and drew my weapon."

"What the fuck you drew yo' weapon for? You was gon' kill yo' own cousin? You was gon' kill my only son?" Shantell asked aggressively.

"Of course not. He just caught me off guard. Drawing my weapon was out of pure instinct."

"What'chu mean, he caught you off guard? Did you see my son shooting?"

"No, but——"

"But my ass! Why did you even pull him over?"

"His tint wasn't legal. The car looked suspicious."

"Suspicious?" Shantell questioned. "I think it's best that you leave, like right now!" warned Shantell.

"I understand. I didn't tell anybody that he fired shots, but he does have a warrant for resisting arrest."

Khufu

Shantell ice grilled Shameeka before slamming the door in her face. She then sat on the sofa and called Khafre.

***

Khafre was in Paradise Park, backed in by the waterfall with Chocolate's head bobbing up and down in his lap.

"That's it, sssss… Shit! Eat that shit up," encouraged Khafre as he gripped Chocolate's hair. She sucked and moaned, curling Khafre's toes until his phone rang. He looked and saw that it was his mother calling. "Aye, hold up, stop for a minute."

"Mm…mmm!" moaned Chocolate, not wanting to stop.

Khafre snatched her head from his lap and answered the phone. "What's up, Ma?"

"Khafre, I need to talk to you. Can you come by?" Shantell asked with a tone of importance.

"I'm a li'l caught up right now, Ma. What's good doe? You can talk to me, ma," Khafre stated, pushing Chocolate's head away as she was trying to put Khafre back in her mouth.

"Yo' cousin came by here looking for you."

"Which one, Momma?"

"The one who used to work at the county jail. I guess she is patrolling the streets now."

"Who, Shameeka?"

"Yeah! She said that she pulled you over, and you took her on a foot chase. She say you fired some shots too."

"I'on know nothing about all that. I'ma talk to you in a li'l bit," Khafre stated, not wanting to talk over the phone.

"Okay. Be careful. She say you got a warrant for resisting arrest."

"That's all?"

"Yeah, that's the only charge."

"A'ight, Mom. Thanks."

"Okay, I love you."

"Love you too, Ma." Khafre hung up the phone. Chocolate attempted to put Khafre's dick back in her mouth, but he pushed her away and put it back in his joggers.

"Ugh! Why, you trippin'? And why the hell you got them gloves on?" asked Chocolate.

"Cuz it's cold, girl. Ma, reach in the glove box and roll that weed up."

"Boy, I don't know how to roll no blunt," replied Chocolate, child-like.

"You gon' learn, tonight. It's plenty of blunts in there."

"What'chu gonna give me if I do?" asked Chocolate as she opened the glove box.

"One up top."

Khafre put a bullet in the side of Chocolate's head, slumping her in the passenger's seat. KD's and Sito's bodies hand been found behind the Beer Hut on 13th Street by a smoker. Word had quickly spread around town that Sito was seen last with Chocolate. Not leaving nothing to chance, Khafre made his mind up to get rid of her.

He got out of the stolen Buick, walked around the corner and hopped in his Audi. He then drove off into the night, adding another soul beneath his belt.

Khufu

CHAPTER 21
TO FAMILY

The weather was dreary when Khafre pulled into Offtop's driveway a little after twelve p.m. He had just finished smoking a blunt of purple and was putting the roach out in the ashtray when his phone rang.

"Yeah, what up?"

"Damn, that's how you do me?" asked Jade briskly.

"What'chu mean, li'l one?"

"You and ya li'l white girls take me down through there, and I'on here nothing from you in days. That's what we doing?" Khafre laughed before replying.

"Nall, ma, it ain't like that. I'm out here, moving around. You know how that shit, go."

"Well, when you gon' find time to move around this way? I miss you," whined Jade.

"I'ma pull up on ya."

"I hope sooner rather than later."

"Patience, li'l one." Khafre's phone beeped. He looked to see who the other caller was. "Look, I'm onto something right now. Give me a few, you will smell me in a minute," proclaimed Khafre.

"You promise?"

"Indeed."

"Okay, I'm here."

Khafre clicked over to the other caller. "Yeah, who is this?"

"This Cowboy."

"Nigga, how the fuck you get my number?"

"Baby girl shot it to me."

Khafre made a mental note to check Lexus for giving his number out. "You ain't scared to call me?"

"For what?" Cowboy replied.

Khafre chuckled. "What's on ya mind?"

"That hoe gone man. I'm through fucking her," stated Cowboy, referring to the brick of fentanyl.

"Already?"

"Yeah, that hoe pussy was tight work too. I need you to pull up on me, or I can come to you. How you wanna do it?"

Knowing that he killed one of Cowboy's associates, Khafre had it in mind that Cowboy might be setting play in motion for retaliation. He decided to spin him for now,

"Give me a few days. I'ma hit'chu back," Khafre assured as he noticed his auntie standing in the doorway.

"Okay, no problem. Get at me."

Khafre hung the phone up and got out of his car. He approached his auntie, who was smiling from ear to ear and hugged her neck.

"Heyyy, Auntie's baby. You been alright?'" asked CC.

"Yeah, I've been coolin', Auntie."

"Yo' uncle in there talking to the boys. You hungry?"

"I'm good, thank you doe," said Khafre, entering the house.

"Okay, I guess I'll talk to you later. I'm finna go lay my ass down."

"A'ight, Auntie."

"Love you, baby."

"Love you too," Khafre replied before walking to his cousin's room.

Before he went there, he could hear Offtop talking to Hezron and Machi. He didn't want to walk in and intrude on their conversation, so he stayed in the hallway eavesdropping.

"Nah, I done told y'all asses, stay from 'round Khafre! He got too much shit going on in the streets. Everything around him gets killed, and I ain't havin' that wit' y'all."

"Man, that's our cousin!" Hezron replied defensively.

"I'on give a fuck 'bout none of that shit you talking. Stay from around him. You can see him when he come over here."

After hearing that, Khafre eased out of the hallway and had a seat in the living room. He helped himself to a shot of Remy and sparked a pre-rolled blunt that was on the table. *Damn. This nigga ain't got a problem sending me to put a hole in a nigga's head, but don't want his sons out there with me. What type of biased shit this nigga on?* Khafre thought as he gazed at the ceiling, blowing smoke.

"Damn, nephew! How long have you been here?" asked Offtop oddly.

"I just walked in, Unc," lied Khafre, passing Offtop the blunt.

"You ain't call me. I thought I was gon' have to cancel the contracts."

"Nall, don't ever do that. You know I'm on go."

Offtop pulled from the blunt then exhaled. "Already."

"So, what'chu got for me?" Khafre retorted, downing his shot of Remy.

"Hold up, give me a minute," proclaimed Offtop, getting up and heading to the back of the house.

Moments later, Hezron and Machi came into the living room.

"What up, Cuz?" greeted Hezron.

"What up, fam" added Machi.

"What up, family?" asked Khafre, dapping both of his cousins up.

"We coolin'," said Machi.

"Man, I gotta holla at'chu !" exclaimed Hezron.

"A'ight. Y'all thought about what we talked 'bout?" asked Khafre.

"Yeah, we gon get at'chu 'bout that later," assured Machi.

"Y'all go back in the room while we talk," ordered Offtop.

"I'ma call you, Cuz." Machi started heading to his room.

"Love you, fam," Hezron insisted, following behind Machi.

"Love you too," replied Khafre.

Offtop sat next to Khafre and handed him a folder. Khafre opened it and examined its contents. There were two contracts. Khafre closed the folder, set it on the table, and nodded his head up and down, solidifying his acceptance of the contracts. He then poured two shots for him and Offtop.

"Let's make a toast, Unc."

"What we toasting to?" asked Offtop, raising his shot glass.

Khafre raised his glass.

"To my family!"

Khufu

CHAPTER 22
NOT MY NIGGAS

It was a sunny day in Atlanta. The streets were active, and the women were fully formed and majestic. Khafre was in awe on how the women really were succulent like peaches. Never experiencing life beyond Florida, he was captivated by the ambience. It was a paradise away from the vile and parasitic streets of Fort Pierce, where the population was only forty-five-thousand.

Khafre sat strategically in a murder bucket, parked outside of Wendy's on Martin Luther King and Fulton Industrial Boulevard. He peered through a pair of 8 x 21 compact binoculars as he spotted his victim coming out of the halfway house on Windell Court. The prey made his way to Fulton Industrial and hopped in a 220 Nissan Rogue that was parked at a gas station. Khafre trailed him slyly and had to make a quick U-turn when his victim stopped to pick up a prostitute. He then followed him up what appeared to be a hill type road that contained a lot of warehouses. Eager to be enveloped by a woman's touch after five years, the victim, whose name was Kilo, didn't even notice death in his rear view. He pulled behind an un-occupied warehouse and parked his vehicle. Khafre parked on the side of the warehouse, pulled out a burner phone, and dialed his mother's number. She picked up on the third ring.

"Who the hell is this?" Shantell asked aggressively.

Khafre laughed before replying. "This is me, Momma."

"Me who?"

"You got some more kids I'on know about?"

"Boy, I know this you. What's up? How's Momma's baby doing?"

"I'm working right now. I just called to see if you got all my bank account information for my yacht cleaning bidness. I had my bidness partners send it to you yesterday."

"Yeah, I got it. Your business partners sound like they white. Where did you meet them at?"

"Touch both sides of ya nose," laughed Khafre.

"Boy, who you think you talking to?"

"I ain't got the time right now, Momma. You got all the clients and website information. Make sure you run my bidness properly. If I hear anything, I'ma fire that ass!"

Shantell chucked. "Why you sent me all that? Where are you going?"

"That's in case something happens. I love you, Momma. Gotta go."

"Khafre, what——"

Click!

Khafre stepped out of the murder bucket and peeked around the warehouse. Once he saw the Nissan rocking back and forth, he rounded the building and quickly closed the distance between him and the car. When he opened the door, Kilo had the prostitute's legs over his shoulders. He was so into it, that he didn't even hear the door open. The prostitute leaned over to look behind Kilo and found herself staring through the barrel of a nickel Rosewood Glock 30. Her eyes bugged as she attempted to use Kilo for cover, but Khafre planted one in her left eye. He put the remaining twelve shots in the back of Kilo's head and back, then calmly walked back to his getaway car.

Khafre lit a blunt and made his way back down Fulton Industrial, then headed to MLK, where he drove into Charlie Brown's airport and pulled into a hanger. He then went out and made his way to a private plane that awaited him. Khafre boarded the plane and flew back to Fort Pierce.

The hit was for a Colombian named Guach, who moved from Colombia to Atlanta in Fayetteville. Kilo had snitched on Gaucho's son and got him a life sentence in the feds. Guach had met Offtop through his nephew Pedro, who was one of Offtop's plugs in high grade weed. The hit was for one-hundred bands. Khafre would get half of that.

***

Headed to Orlando, Khafre had managed to avoid any contact from law enforcement, riding with a M4 Carbine on the passenger seat. He got off on exit 528, took it to Interstate 4, and got off on Kirkman. Khafre thought of his underprivileged childhood as he passed by Universal Studios and made a right on Old Winter Garden Road, then a left on Quntar Road, which brought him to Hopes Circle, a hood known as 300. It had earned its name from putting in the most work with less people. The leader was a dopeboy by the name of Montana. Offtop and Montana knew each other through business. Montana presented the contracts to Offtop, who promised to have them executed.

Khafre pulled into Judy's Diner, parked, and waited for his signal. Montana sat inside the diner and enjoyed a plate of grits, eggs, and corned beef hash. Two of his workers sat across from him, pigging out on steak and eggs. Montana grabbed a napkin and wiped his mouth before speaking.

"Y'all boys enjoying the meal?" asked Montana washing his food down with a glass of orange juice.

"Hell yeah," replied Lade.

"Yeah, this shit good," added Rambo.

"Breakfast at Judy's is always good. You know what ain't good? Work missing. Money coming up short. Ain't nothin' good 'bout that. Any one of y'all know anything 'bout that?"

Lade grabbed his iced tea and took long, slow sips to avoid the question.

"Nall, Montana, we don't know nothin' 'bout that, "replied Rambo, breaking eye contact.

"What about chu, Lade?"

"Come on, Montana. You put me on. I wouldn't play you like that," Lade assured.

"You know what? Y'all right, I must be trippin'. We been homies since snotty noses. I prolly miscounted and forgot who I fronted that work to." Montana rubbed his hand over his bald head. "Damn, this corned beef hash running right through me. Y'all boys excuse me for a minute," Montana enunciated, getting up and heading to the restroom.

"Man, he know we took that shit," Lade stated, voice tense and hysterical.

"Nigga, shut the fuck up," replied Rambo through clenched teeth. "You so fucking, scary. That nigga ain't going to do shit."

"I'on know, man," muttered Lade.

A man entered the diner in all black YSL T-shirt and sweatpants, with a YSL Covid mask. The mysterious man headed straight in Lade and Rambo's direction.

"Fuck is up with this nigga?" asked Rambo shifting in his seat.

Khafre lifted the M4 Carbine that was concealed under his YSL sweater.

"What up, niggas?"

Khafre put three hot ones in Lade, then lined Rambo up, who attempted to reach for his pistol.

BOC!BOC!BOC!BOC!BOC!

Rambo slumped over in an awkward position with his pistol clutched in his hand. Khafre sauntered out of the diner collectively, got in his ride and pulled away. Moments later, Montana returned from the restroom and put on an Oscar award winning performance until the ambulance and police came.

"Oh Lord! Not my niggas! Why, Jesus, Lord, God noooo!"

CHAPTER 23
YOU TALK TO MUCH

Hezron had called Khafre's phone for the fourth time and got the voicemail again. *Why this nigga ain't pickin' up the fuckin' phone?* thought Hezron as he a made right on 25th and Avenue D.

"Shit! Bitch, watch yo' teeth when you sucking my shit, hoe," warned Hezron.

Amber took her mouth off of Hezron's dick for a moment.

"I'm not using my teeth, bae!" exclaimed Amber, rolling hard on molly. She attempted to put her mouth back on Hezron.

"Watch out! I'm straight!" Hezron pushed Ambers away from him.

"Just sit yo' ass back in that seat. Look at'cha grinding your teeth and shit. Hoe, you tweaking!" Hezron took a pull from his blunt.

"Whateva! I'on say nothing 'bout all that weed you be smokin'. You'll give a nigga the shirt off yo' back for a blunt," Amber retorted, reaching for Hezron's blunt. He slapped her hand away.

"Hoe, stop flaggin'. A nigga can't even spend the night at'cha house and wake up to a decent bowl of cereal, hoe! Roaches crawling all out the box and shit!"

"I ain't got no damn roaches," lied Amber.

"Shittin' me!" added Hezron, making a left on Avenue D and 21st. "What the fuck?" muttered Hezron, pulling over in front of Smitty's.

"Don't tell people I got roaches."

"Shut the fuck up! Here!" Hezron handed Amber the blunt. "Stay yo' ass in the car," Hezron ordered, hopping out of his tinted-up Kia that he drove whenever he wanted to be low-key. Hezron approached KC, who was in the door frame of his car, talking on the phone with his back turned.

"What up, nigga?" asked Hezron.

When KC turned to see who was behind him, Hezron slapped him in the face with a Springfield .45, dropping him. Hezron stood over KC with his pistol pointed directly in the middle of his head.

"Where the fuck my money at, nigga!"

KC's eyes grew in size, but he gave no answer.

Hezron put two in KC's head and trotted back to his whip. He got in and pulled off.

"What'chu shoot that boy fa?" questioned Amber.

"I ain't shoot, nobody. Shut up and sit back."

"I just saw you."

Hezron pointed his pistol at Amber.

"Get that shit out my face, boy!" Amber said, moving the gun from her face. "I ain't gon' say, shit. Just tell me."

Hezron gazed at her for a moment before speaking. "He owe me."

"How much?"

"Two pounds."

"You shot that boy over two pounds? And you say I'm tweaking."

"Shut the fuck up!"

Amber gazed at Hezron before replying.

"They still ain't find out, who killed my baby daddy. Was it you?"

"I'on know nothing about that. Matter of fact..."Hezron pulled his dick out, grabbed Amber by her hair, and put his dick in her mouth. "Hoe, you talk too damn much."

***

"Damn, girl," Machi moaned, gripping Crystal's butter soft ass cheeks as she rode him fervently.

"Oooh-weeee, boy... Sss...damn!" groaned Crystal as she placed her hands on Machi's chest, leaned forward, and began to bounce on his dick rapidly.

"Ride that dick," Machi encouraged, meeting her thrust for thrust.

"Ooohh... Yesss, I'm finna... Sss... Oooww... I'm cumming!"

Machi lifted Crystal off his dick and placed her on his face.

"Oooww, you so nasty!" cried Crystal as she grinded on Machi's tongue and released her nectar.

After tasting her, he flipped Crystal on her back then entered her eagerly. He got in push up position, with the intention of stroking Crystal into a blissful oblivious state, but was mistaken. Every stroke that Machi delivered, no matter which way, Crystal met him halfway. His mind boggled at how Crystal was fucking him from the bottom.

"Fuuucck!" yelled Machi as he released into Crystal's hot wet pussy.

"Yeesss, cum in this pussy, daddy!" Crystal cried as she came right behind him.

Machi pulled out of her and rolled over on his back, galvanized by the after effect of his orgasm.

"Whooo! That was so good," Crystal admitted.

"You fuckin' right," Machi agreed.

Crystal wrapped one of her legs around Machi's body and began rubbing on his chest. Machi ran his hand through her natural long hair.

"I can't believe we just did that."

"Believe it," Machi retorted.

"So, what this mean? What now?"

"What'chu want it to mean?" asked Machi.

Crystal shrugged her shoulders. "I'on know," asserted Crystal, still rubbing on Machi's chest. "Just let this shit grow into whatever it's gon' be."

"Okay." Machi's phone rang. He looked and saw it was his brother Hezron. "What's up, brah?"

"Where you at?" asked Hezron.

"I'm ducked off. What's good?"

"You seen or heard from Khafre? I've been calling him with no answer," stressed Hezron.

"Nall, I ain't seen him. I'm finna call 'em now. Hold on." Machi clicked over and dialed Khafre's number, then merged the calls.

"You have reached the voicemail box of Khafre..."

"See what I'm talking 'bout?" exclaimed Hezron.

"Calm down, brah. What'chu need to talk to him about?"

"You ain't gonna believe this shit, bro. I'm finna send you a text message, hold up."

Moments later, Machi received the message from Hezron. "What the fuck!"

"Now you see why am I looking for him?"

"What's wrong bae?" Crystal asked, concerned.

"Nothing, ma. Aye, brah, I'm getting dressed right now. Meet me at Auntie Shantell's house. I know she knows where Cuz at."

"A'ight, nigga, I'm headed there now," replied Hezron, hanging up the phone.

"Machi, baby, tell me what's going on please."

"It's best if you don't know. I'ma call you later."

CHAPTER 24
YOUNG BLOOD

"So how my bidness been running, Mama?" Khafre asked with his back against the wall while observing the movement of inmates. After executing the two contracts, Khafre turned himself in. Instead of bonding out, he decided to take thirty days for resisting arrest.

"Business is running smoothly. I hired a few Mexicans. They work good, and they cheaper. I got two clients lined up for tomorrow at the marina."

"That's what I love to hear. Money, money, yeahhh, yeahhh!" clowned Khafre, impersonating Bernie Mack from *The Player's Club*.

"Boy, you are so crazy." Shantell laughed. "Hanna and Samantha asked about you."

"Aye, I need to make an important phone call!" stated an inmate named Big Twank.

Khafre held up one hand, letting Big Twank know that he would be off the phone shortly.

"Who was that?" Shantell asked, concerned.

"Nobody, Ma. That's my homie playing around. What Hanna and Samantha hollerin' 'bout?"

"They just told me to tell you to call them."

"Oh yeah? Check this out, Ma. I'ma call you later. I'm finna call them right now. I love you, lady."

"Okay, baby, I love you too." Khafre hung up the phone. "Aye, bro. Phone. I told you I wasn't gon' be long!" Khafre exclaimed, handing Big Twank the phone.

"Ain't no pressure, brah. I just gotta catch my girl at a certain time," explained Big Twank, grabbing the phone.

"Over stood brah," replied Khafre.

Big Twank turned to dial the number.

"Aye, nigga!"

Twank turned around and caught a straight right to the chin. His brain rattled before he dropped to the stained concrete floor. "Bitch-ass nigga!" Khafre proclaimed seethingly before dragging Twank to the first cell closest to the phone, where he proceeded to pummel Twank to a bloody, unconscious state.

"Come on, young blood. That's enough."

Khafre looked up and saw an old head standing at the front of the cell. He stomped on Twank's head once more, then walked out of the cell. He then grilled the old head before walking to his cell. Moments later, the old head came to Khafre's cell and stood at the entrance.

"Fuck you want, nigga? You good?" Khafre asked warily.

"Be cool, young blood. I just wanna talk to you. Let me get a minute."

"Talk, nigga."

"Not in here, young blood. Come out here, let's grab a table," suggested the old head as he took a seat at the table, which was out of earshot from other inmates.

Khafre followed and had as seat across from him. "What up?" Khafre asked impatiently.

"You recognize me?"

"Nall, nigga."

"I'm Biggs."

"Okay, what's next?" Khafre stated, unimpressed.

"Listen, I've been watching you since you came in. I like how you move, young blood, so I'ma keep it all the way funky wit'chu. You know a nigga named Lotto?"

Biggs had Khafre's attention now. "What about that nigga?" Khafre retorted.

"He put a check on your head."

Khafre laughed. "Tell 'em good luck with that."

"I'm the one he appointed to cash that check."

Khafre laughed again. "Fuck outta here wit' that shit." Seconds later, Khafre saw that Biggs was serious.

"You killed his cousin, Kurt."

"I'on know what'chu talkin' about," replied Khafre defensively.

"Everybody knows you did, young blood. You Khafre, right?"

Khafre sat in silence and stared into Bigg's eyes.

122

"I have been following you for weeks, but you have always been on point. Remember, I was following you in the projects in that Impala? You hopped out and put multiple bullet holes in in my shit, remember?"

Khafre's jaw tensed as his adrenaline started pumping rigorously.

"Calm down, young blood. I'm trying to make shit right wit'chu."

"How the fuck you doin' that?"

"I'm a reasonable man. For the right price, we can reverse the hit," proposed Biggs.

Khafre's face turned hard as granite. "Reverse the hit?" Khafre caught himself and thought clearly before responding. His frown turned into a devilish smirk. "Yeah, Yeah, we can do that."

"My man," Biggs replied, shaking Khafre's hand to seal the deal.

Khufu

CHAPTER 25
KILLA FA REAL

Khafre sat on the steps of an abandoned building on Avenue T and smoked a blunt of Mango Kush. Unbeknownst to Khafre, it was the same building where his father, Baby G, left his uncle Mundo half dead. Khafre's thoughts were all over the place when his phone rang.

"What up wit' it?" answered Khafre.

"How have you been? I haven't heard from you in a while!" exclaimed Jarrod.

"Yeah, I know. I have been puttin' in work. You know how that goes."

"What about the situation I gave you? You did your thing yet?" Jarrod questioned, referring to the brick of fentanyl.

"Not yet. I got some shit that needs to be handled before I jump into that."

"Understood. Do you need anything?"

"I'm cool. You are appreciated though."

"Anytime, man. Listen, when you do get around to that, I got more for you. So just hit me when you ready."

"Already."

When Khafre hung up the phone, a gray '87 Fleetwood pulled into the driveway. Moments later, Biggs got out of the car and gave Khafre a confirmation look. Khafre nodded his head. Bigs went to his trunk, popped it, then pulled Lotto out of it. He then brought him to face Khafre.

"Lotto! What the lick read, homie?" Khafre smiled. "You don't look too happy to see me," Khafre stated, snatching the tape off of the Lotto's mouth.

"Fuck!" cried Lotto.

"I heard you put a check on my head. Is that true?" Khafre questioned, his brows creased with curiosity.

"You fucking right I did, pussy! You killed my cousin!" Lotto retorted, voice quavering.

125

"That's what they say." Khafre smirked. "What about yo' fine-ass sister? They tell you I put her in that wheelchair, too?"

Lotto spit in Khafre's face. Off impulse, Khafre threw a right hook and dropped Lotto to his knees.

"Pick his ass up and get 'em in here," demanded Khafre.

Biggs planted his pistol in the back of Lotto's head and followed Khafre into the bando.

BOC!

BOC!

BOC!

BOC!

BOC!

Hezron put four RIP rounds into Biggs' legs, dropping him, causing his pistol to slide a few feet away from him. Lotto flinched and tucked his head, thinking he was hit. Machi raised his FNH .40 and planted three hot ones in Lotto's chest, knocking him down with his hands still tied behind his back.

BOC!

BOC!

Khafre put two more holes in Lotto's torso, then stood over Biggs and pointed his FN57 at his chest.

"I thought, we had an agreement, young blood," moaned Biggs

"The fuck I look like paying you to touch a nigga? I'm a killa, for real!" Khafre proclaimed, biting his bottom lip.

BOC!

BOC!

BOC!

BOC!

Khafre put four Hornady Hollow rounds in Biggs' chest.

"Stupid nigga!" Khafre asserted as he stood and watched Lotto and Biggs clutch on their chests until exhaling their last breaths.

"What'chu wanna do, Cuz?" asked Hezron.

"Put them niggas on them tables over there," Khafre instructed, pointing his pistol towards two tables in the living room. Hezron and Machi laid Biggs and Lotto side by side.

"Damn! This nigga Lotto heavy as hell," Machi said, breathing heavy.

"Chill. I'ma take 'bout eight pounds off these niggas in a minute," stated Khafre as he headed to the first room on the left, went into the doorless closet, and grabbed a band saw. He returned seconds later with an odious smirk on his face.

"What'chu finna do, fam?" questioned Machi.

Khafre turned the band saw on, and positioned it over Lotto's neck. "You put a check on my head, huh?" Khafre muttered through clenched teeth as he placed the saw on Lotto's neck and watched it cut smooth as butter. Lotto's head fell and rolled oddly on the floor.

"Damn, Cuz! Let me do the other nigga!" Hezron said excitedly while Machi turned his head, trying not to vomit.

"Let me find out, you got them li'l baby guts," Khafre clowned Machi before handing Hezron the saw.

"Bitch ass nigga!" Hezron cut Lotto's head off. He laughed petulantly when Bigg's head rolled next to Lotto's.

"Put the saw down, nigga," Khafre demanded. Hezron did as he was told. Khafre picked up two spikes that were connected to a chain and grabbed a hammer. He then hammered a spike into each head.

"What'chu on, Cuz?" questioned Hezron.

Khafre handed Hezron a garbage bag. "Nigga, hold this bag open." Khafre pulled out his phone and dialed an old friend.

"Sak-ap-fet!" Haitian Baby yelled into the phone.

"What's up, Haitian Baby? This Khafre."

"Been a long time, goon," Haitian Baby retorted excitedly. "What the lick read?"

"I got something for ya."

"Say no more. Drop the addy."

Khafre hung the phone up.

"Aye, fam, I got some shit to show you," Hezron stated pulling his phone out and scrolling down Facebook.

Khafre grabbed the phone, gazed at what Hezron wanted him to see, and shook his head in disbelief.

***

"Hello?" answered Jade

"What's good, beautiful?"

"Khafre?"

"Who else?"

"Boy, it's four thirty in the morning. And why you calling me from a different number?"

"You ain't happy to hear from me? You don't miss a nigga?"

"Of course I do."

"Well, kill all that other shit and come outside."

"Outside?"

"Yeah, I'm out chere. Come sit on this dick real quick."

Jade got up and peered out of her blinds. "Your ass is out here, for real!" Jade exclaimed, smiling.

"I'm finna pull off on yo' ass," Khafre threatened.

"Don't do that. I'm coming now," assured Jade, hanging up the phone and opening up her door. She smiled then made her way towards the Cadillac.

"Heyyy baby," Jade whined seductively. Just as she made it to the passenger window, she noticed something swinging above her head. She stopped to get a good look and saw that there were two heads swinging on a powerline like a pair of old Reebok classics.

"What the fuck is that?" Jade asked, perplexed.

"Oh, that's just the nigga Lotto and Biggs hanging out."

Jade took her attention off of the heads and glanced at Khafre. He lifted the same FN-57 that he hit Biggs with and planted one in Jade's forehead, killing her instantly, leaving her mouth and eyes open. Khafre pulled off calmly and headed to Taylors Creek to dump the car and murder weapon.

Hezron had showed Khafre a photo of Jade standing in between Lotto and Biggs. It was mandatory that she die.

CHAPTER 26
YOU TALKING STUPID

Khafre had followed his mark to an undisclosed location that he wasn't familiar with. He was parked a few houses down. Watching him though a pair of binoculars, Khafre saw that he seemed to be engaged in a deep conversation on his phone. Khafre waited patiently while having a conversation of his own with his cousins. He had Hezron and Machi on speaker phone.

"So, what up wit'chu niggas? Y'all thought about gettin' this money wit' me or nall?"

"Yeah, we thought 'bout it," Machi stated. "I got something I gotta handle before I get into that," Machi replied.

"Shid, I'm ready now! But I'm waiting on my brother," Hezron added.

"Damn, you need permission from Machi to get money?" Khafre retorted sardonically.

"I ain't moving without my brother!" Hezron stated firmly.

"A'ight. I'ma move, without chu niggas. It'll be there when y'all get'cha minds right. I'm on one right no. Hit me later." Khafre hung up the phone. He then stepped out of his stolen Buick in a wig and a dress, then sauntered into a yard that was three houses down, clutching a Fendi purse. Once he reached the back of the house, he jumped three fences, calmly walked up to a window and shattered it with pieces of spark plugs. He pushed the window in, then climbed in.

Five minutes later, Khafre's victim could be heard entering the house. Khafre reached into the purse and drew a FN-509 with a suppressor. His mark entered the room across from him. The sound of a trash bag could be heard, followed by a money machine beeping. Khafre crept out of the room he was in and entered the one across the hall where his target sat with his back turned.

"So, this where you keep it at, huh?" Khafre asked, gazing at stacks of money.

"Ahh!" The scared man jumped, then turned around with his hands up.

"What up, nigga?" Khafre implored with a single tear cascading down his right cheek.

"Nephew? What the fuck you doing? Fuck you dressed like that for? Man, put the gun down, and stop playing."

"You know I'on play games, Unc."

"So, what is this? You came here to rob me? Huh? You gon' bite the hand that feeds you?"

"Nall. I'on want shit else from you, Unc! I'ma leave all this shit in there wit' yo' brains and blood stained on it."

"All I did was be there for you, nephew."

"The last time I was at your house, I heard that shit you were telling your sons."

Offtop put his head down briefly, then tried to explain.

"Shut the fuck up!" Khafre demanded through clenched teeth. "How the fuck you ain't got a problem sending my father's only son to fill the streets with blood, but got a problem when yours do? Huh? You don't want my cousins around me, huh? You told my cousins everything around me dies, right? How the fuck I'on know, that you the one who sent Archie to kill my pops? I mean, you've been operating for years, and you ain't never been busted."

"You talking stupid now," added Offtop.

"Am I? Cuz the shit, making a whole lot of sense to me. My pops told me everything before he passed. He wanted to kill Auntie CC before she made it right wit' him. You could have been, still feeling some kind of way 'bout that!" Khafre exclaimed.

"Put the gun down, nephew."

"I ain't yo' fuckin' nephew, nigga!"

FOP!

FOP!

FOP!

FOP!

Khafre put four holes in Offtop's head. He dropped whatever was left of his head on top of the garbage bag full of money. His blood ran from his head and stained all the money in the bag. Khafre calmly walked out of the front door down to the stolen vehicle and drove away.

CHAPTER 27
WE OUT'CHERE

It was a beautiful sunny day, yet a disheartening one. Those who loved and did business with Offtop mourned as CC sent him off in style. Instead of having a funeral, the whole city came out to pay their respect to Offtop as he sat in the driveway of one of his traps in a Lamborghini Aventador with the door up. CC made sure that he had on all his jewelry, rings on every finger, as he gripped the steering wheel in Maison Margiela from head to toe. She even made sure that his face bore a smile, showing his VV'S dancing in the sunlight. Machi and Hezron stood guard strapped with vests and Glocks to make sure nobody snatched their father's jewelry. Khafre consoled CC as she stood off to the side, trying to keep it together.

"I just can't understand who would wanna kill him? He gave everybody more than fair prices. He fronted people work, even after they fucked the pack up. Anybody could have got anything from him!" cried CC.

"It prolly was a hit, Auntie. It had to be personal, cuz they ain't take the money," Khafre stated apathetically.

"Nobody knows about that stash house. Shit, I didn't know 'bout it. This hit just doesn't make no sense to me." CC added, shaking her head in disbelief.

"Maybe he led a secret life away from home, Auntie."

"It's possible. Now that he is gone, I'on know what I'ma do. He just got a big shipment from his plug the day before he died. His plug asking me to take over, but my mind ain't into that shit right now," CC said removing a blunt and sparking it.

"What about Hezron and Machi?" Khafre inquired.

"They don't know about it. I haven't told 'em. I don't want them out there. They father left enough money to secure the future. We good on money."

"What'chu gon' do, with the shipment?"

"You askin like you want it, nephew," CC pronounced passing half the blunt.

"What da weight is?"

"A thousand pounds of exotic."

"I'll take 'em off your hands."

"You got some money put up?"

"I gotta li'l something put up."

"Give me one hunnid thousand, they yours."

Khafre did the math in his head quickly. He realized that even if he let them go for two-thousand apiece, that was two million.

"I call that, Auntie," he confirmed, passing CC back the blunt.

"Just call me in a few weeks. I'll let'chu know where to meet me at. Don't say nothing to your cousins."

"I'm on point, Auntie."

"A'ight, go over there wit'cha cousins and make sure nobody reach into that car."

"A'ight. Keep yo' head up, Auntie, You know I love you."

"Love you too, nephew."

Khafre walked over to where Machi and Hezron were. There was a barrier that was twenty feet away from the lambo that Offtop was in to keep the onlookers at bay. Gangstas, hustlers, and a plethora of women all crowded around the barrier, poured liquor and smoke big blunts one last time with the Trap King Of The City.

"What's good? Y'all boys a'ight?" Khafre asked.

"When we find out who crossed our pops, we will be," Machi stated.

"You already know. Y'all rode with me when my pops got killed. I'm front line wit'cha!"

"I'm smoking everything moving," Hezron added.

"I know this is a bad time to ask, but y'all boys ready to move that fent?"

"Fuck it! !" exclaimed Hezron.

"It's whateva, fam," added Machi.

"Let's set this bitch on fire, then," Khafre retorted.

CHAPTER 28
DISLOYAL-ASS NIGGA

Two months later, Machi and Hezron had the whole city saturated with fentanyl. They opened a trap house in Sunland Gardens, moving two hundred dollar grams. Khafre had put a three on each brick, turning one into four. When he was done, he had twenty-four bricks of Fentanyl. He kept 18 and gave Machi and Hezron three apiece.

Hezron was outside conducting sales when Crystal pulled up in an Infiniti Q50 and stepped out in a Amid Stellar bodysuit and Paloma Picasso heels, clutching a Fendi bag.

"Get this shit, and get the fuck on!" yelled Hezron to a junkie who tried to bargain for another gram in exchange for a blow job.

"Be nice to your supporters. Without them, you ain't nothing," Crystal stated, approaching, walking delicately in heels.

"Damn, girl, you thick as yesterday's grits. You came to see me?" clowned Hezron.

Crystal smiled. "I'on break up happy homes."

"What'chu mean?"

"Everybody knows you and Amber are in an entanglement. Nah, stop playing and go get Machi."

"Machi ain't here," Hezron lied.

"His car right there. Boy, I ain't got time for yo' li'l games," Crystal enunciated as she walked past Hezron into the trap house. When she entered the spot, bottles of Patron, cigar guts, and Brown Store chicken boxes littered the living room.

"Machi!" Crystal yelled as she made her way through the hall.

"Beat, this pussy, nigga! Sss.... Fuck me! Yes! Nigga, shit! Right there! Right there! Shit! Don't stop! Shit, I'm cummin'!"

When Crystal approached the door, it was cracked. She pushed it open and was surprised to see Machi with Tweet's legs pinned behind her head, stroking her. Crystal's heart sank into the pit of the stomach and filled with rage. She rushed Machi, pushing him out of Tweet's pussy. By the time Machi realized what was taking place, Crystal was all over Tweet punitively. Tweet curled up in an attempt to stop the onslaught, but to no avail.

Khufu

"Da fuck is you doing?" Machi asked in a drunken, slur reaching to stop Crystal from beating Tweet to death.

"Don't fucking touch me!" Crystal screamed as she laid off of Tweet and picked up the Fendi bag that she had dropped when she entered the room. She reached in her bag, drew a Baby pocket rocket .25 FN, and pointed it at Machi's face. "Back the fuck up, you disloyal-ass nigga!" Crystal could smell the weed and liquor on Machi's breath. She knew Machi's father had just died, but that was no excuse for betraying her. Just the thought of it all sent her over the edge. Crystal jumped back in the bed and pistol-whipped Tweet unconscious. Once satisfied, she put one in the head of her .25 and aimed it between Tweet's eyes.

"Don't do that shit, Crystal," Hezron advised, standing in the doorway. "Think about yo' daughter. Come on now, that hoe ain't worth it," asserted Hezron, grabbing Crystal's shoulder and pulling her back.

She gazed at Machi with resentment in her heart, then turned to walk away.

"Crystal!" yelled Machi. "Crystal, come here!"

Crystal ignored Machi and headed to her car with Hezron behind her.

"Thank you, Hezron. I almost threw my life away over nothing."

"No problem. You owe me a shot of ass now," Hezron joked, trying to make her smile.

"Bye, Hezron!" Crystal retorted, getting in her car. She pulled off in tears.

CHAPTER 29
AUNTIE!

Khafre had just met up with Cowboy and given him four bricks. Cowboy paid him for two and got two on consignment. He'd convinced Khafre that he had no ill will toward him about the mishaps that transpired at his trailer. Both parties agreed to get money and do respectable business. Cowboy assured Khafre that he'd be in touch in a week or two.

Khafre was now headed to meet his auntie CC in a U-Haul to pick up the shipment when he got a call. He saw that it was the twins.

"Hey babies," greeted Khafre, answering the phone.

"Heyyy, daddy, we miss you!" whined Hanna.

"Yeah, we miss you, daddy!" Samantha added.

"I miss my babies too. Where ya at?"

"We just got back from Europe. We wanna come see you, we have something important to tell you!" Samantha exclaimed.

"Okay, give me a few days. I'ma call y'all back. I'm on something right now," Khafre disclosed, turning into a food bank on US1.

"Okay, just make sure, you call us back, daddy," Hanna said.

"I got'chu." Khafre hung up the phone, then backed the U-Haul next to CC's Benz truck. When he hopped out, CC was smoking a blunt. She offered it to Khafre, but he declined.

"How you doing, nephew?" CC asked mildly.

"I'm a'ight, how 'bout you?" Khafre retorted, hugging CC's neck.

"I'm making it, just trying to live through it, you know."

"Yeah. I know it's hard, but ya gotta keep pushing through the shit that life throw at'chu. Unc getting smacked at his apex in life shows you that you gotta live every day like its ya last," voiced Khafre.

"I hear you, nephew. I just miss him so much," CC replied, turning to go open the door to the food bank. "Come on, let's load this shit up."

Khufu

Khafre followed CC into the food bank. "You got the work in a food bank?"

"Yeah, that's how we get it in. Boxed food gets donated all the time, especially canned goods. Who knows? You might open one and find a pound or two in it." CC laughed.

"Aw, man, that shit genius," Khafre admitted, amazed.

"Your uncle was a genius. Now load this shit up, while nobody's around being nosy and shit."

It took CC and Khafre nearly thirty minutes to load the shipment in the U-Haul.

"Whooooo! You got the butter from the duck tonight, nephew. I'm finna go lay my ass down. You got that money wit'chu, or you gon' pay me later?" CC asked, exhausted.

"I got it right here in the truck, Auntie. Hold up." Khafre reached in the U-Haul. When he approached CC, she was adjusting the air temperature. "Auntie!"

"Yeah, nephew?" answered CC, turning her attention to Khafre. BOC!BOC!BOC!

Khafre put three hot ones in CC's face, leaving her slumped on the steering wheel. She had laid on the horn, but Khafre used his pistol to push her head off of it, causing her body to lay over in the passenger's floorboard under the dash.

"That's for my pops!" Khafre said to his aunty's dead body, then he hopped in the U-Haul and pulled off.

Khafre never forgot when his father Baby G told him about the family's beef. He never forgot the scar that his father showed him on his head that resulted from his auntie putting a bullet in his head. Even though Baby G told Khafre that he and CC had made amends, Khafre had put in his mind that his auntie had to die. He lived by a code: atrocity for atrocity, blood for blood...a life for a life.

136

CHAPTER 30
STOP

After loading the shipment in his apartment, Khafre had a few words with Wholly, the Arab that owned the store. Wholly told Khafre that he should take a break from the streets and offered to take him to Egypt. As bad as Khafre wanted to see the pyramids and the motherland from which his ancestors came, he respectfully decline and asked for a rain check. Khafre then hopped in the G-Wagon that was gifted to him by his father, and headed to the graveyard. He hopped out with a .40 on his hip and a blunt in his mouth, and headed to Nilya's grave.

"What the lick read, big head?" Khafre asked Nilya, blowing smoke from his nose. "I miss yo' ass so fuckin' much. I been foolin around wit' deez li'l green-ass females, but ain't none of them like you. You were a whole different type of breed. A breed like me." Khafre coughed from the high grade weed, beating on his chest.

"I been putting so much shit in the ground that I done lost count, ma. I'on even know what to feel no more about nothing. I just need you here with me. I shoulda protected you, but I failed you, and for that, I'm sorry." Khafre kneeled down and kissed Nilya's tombstone the same way he used to kiss her forehead.

"I love you, big head," he expressed before getting up to leave.

On the way back to his truck, he stopped by his uncle Mundo's grave.

"What dey do, nigga? This yo' nephew Khafre, yo' brother's son. I really wish I got a chance to meet'chu. That way I could put a fuckin' bullet in yo' face myself! Bitch-ass nigga!" Khafre whipped his dick out and pissed on his uncle Mundo's grave. When he was done, he snatched his .40 out.

"I sent you a li'l company last night," Khafre stated, referring to his auntie CC.

BOC!BOC!BOC!

He put three hollow tips in Mundo's tombstone, then jumped in his truck and peeled out.

Khufu

***

Shantell was relaxing comfortably in the living room, smoking a joint and sipping a cup of White Remy, when she got a knock at the door.

"Who the hell knockin' on my damn door?" questioned Shantell, opening the door.

"Come on, ma, you know damn well you ain't got no friends," Khafre joked, walking into the house.

"Boy, watch yo' mouth. Hell wrong wit'chu? And I do have friends."

"Like who?"

"Mercedes!"

"I'll give you that."

"I'm well known around here," bragged Shantell, feeling galvanized from the weed and Remy.

"I hear you, Momma. But all bullshit aside, I gotta talk to you about some real shit," Khafre pronounced, having a seat next to his mother.

"Oh Lord. What is it?"

Khafre exhaled before speaking. "You know before Pop's death, he told me a lot of shit, Momma. Shit I'm positive he didn't tell you."

"I'm listening," Shantell retorted, her interest piqued.

"Did pops ever tell you who shot 'em?"

"No. He just said that he heard whispers about it, but nothing solid."

"It was Auntie CC."

Shantell looked confused. "Why would she do that?" Shantell used her hand for emphasis.

"Back in the day, Uncle Mundo shot Pops. It was hard to recognize the shooter cuz it was dark outside, but Uncle Mundo came to the hospital and told Pops that it was a nigga named C. Pops found out later on after him and Uncle Mundo killed C that it was Uncle Mundo who really shot 'em."

"How did he know it wasn't C?"

"Pops was fuckin C's baby momma. She was in love with Pops, and her loyalty was wit' Pops, so she laced him up."

"Oh yeah?" Shantell added, feeling envious, shaking her head.

"Kill all that. You know every street nigga got a life outside of home. Pops loved you , Momma, you know that. Anyway, come to find out, C was fuckin' Uncle Mundo's bitch, Yona. So, this green-ass nigga Mundo lied to Pops so they could kill C." Khafre shook his head in disgust. "When pops found out, he left Mundo in a bando for dead, but he was found by some kids. He told Auntie CC what Pops did, but forgot to tell her that he was the one who shot Pops. So after a show Pops had at Lawnwood Stadium, Auntie CC acted like something was wrong with her tire and had Pops to check it. I guess you know she hit Pops up and left him for dead."

"That's why she wouldn't answer her phone for me," Shantell added, replaying the event of that night in the mind.

"It gets deeper," Khafre stated, looking his mother in her eyes.

"Just tell me."

"I killed Auntie CC last night," Khafre exclaimed apathetically.

"Are you serious?"

"As a life sentence. Remember I was doing bidness with Offtop?"

"Yeah."

"He played me, so I put dirt on his chest, too."

Shantell exhaled, rubbing her hands through her hair. "What the fuck is wrong wit'chu? You a fucking demon seed!"

"I got twenty-three of your chromosomes, so what does that say bout'chu?"

"I ain't no damn killa."

"Not yet," Khafre replied, pulling out his phone to check the time.

"Boy, you lost your mind."

"Aaahhhh... Fuck!" Stressed, Khafre hung up his phone after realizing he had pocket dialed Hezron's phone. Hezron had heard the whole conversation.

"What?" asked Shantell, worried.

"My phone was on the whole time! I pocket dialed Hezron's phone."

"Oh my God!"

"Listen, go grab all the money you got laying around and pack a bag. I gotta get'chu somewhere safe. I'ma have to kill these niggas. Go! Hurry up!" Khafre ordered, dialing Wholly's number.

He answered on the second ring. "Hello! Khafre, buddy, how is everything?" Wholly asked.

"Listen, Wholly, I need a favor."

"Anything for you, my friend."

"I need you to put my mother in a safe place, away from here, until I deal with a li'l situation."

"When?"

"Tonight."

"Bring her to me, I take care of her for you, buddy."

"A'ight, Wholly man. Thank you. I love you, Ock."

"Love you, buddy." Click!

"Momma, let's go!" Khafre yelled, snatching a Chris Costa Recon .45 from his Palm Angels track pants.

"I'm ready," Shantell assured gripping her bags with panic-stricken eyes.

Khafre opened the door to survey his surroundings. "Come on, Ma."

Khafre led the way with Shantell on his heels. When they reached Khafre's G-Wagon, an unknown vehicle turned the corner suspiciously with Hezron hanging out of the rooftop clutching a M10 with a box clip that held two-hundred and fifty rounds. Khafre pushed his mother behind the truck, then ran towards the vehicle firing. Hezron let multiple rounds go, missing his target, allowing Khafre to get a shot off, hitting Hezron in his shoulder, causing him to drop his weapon and slip back in the car. When the vehicle stopped by Khafre, who was still firing, the driver, Machi let one shot off and found is mark. Khafre caught one to the head and dropped to the pavement, barely living. Machi knew he was a marksman and never missed so he keep going, slipping away into the night.

"Noooo! Not my baby, Lord Jesus, no!" cried Shantell as she ran over to Khafre, whose right leg was kicking in and out as he fought for his life. "Come on, baby! Stay wit' mama!"

"Stop… Stop… Stop…" Khafre moaned as he rubbed his head, flapping blood everywhere.

Shantell realized that Khafre had fallen into a vegetable-like state and panicked.

"Help! Help me, please!"

A neighbor ran outside to assist her. He tried his best to bring Shantell down, then put Khafre in his G-Wagon and took him to Lawnwood Medical.

Khufu

CHAPTER 31
TELL ME SOMETHIN'

Shantell held Khafre's phone as she waited on the doctor to bring her the update on Khafre. It rang, showing Wholly on the screen.

"Hello! Wholly! They shot my baby! They shot my baby in the head, Wholly!" Shantell cried hysterically.

"Oh my goodness! He was supposed to be bringing you to me for safe keeping. Oh my goodness, Khafre! I'll be right there!"

Shantell buried her face in her hands and continued to sob. Moments later, a doctor came out to inform Shantell on Khafre's condition.

"Ms. Sheffield?"

"Yes, please tell me something, Doctor," begged Shantell with tears all over her face.

"I'm sorry, he didn't make it."

***

After the coroner pronounced Khafre dead, he took him down to the morgue. He then filed Khafre as a number, tagged his toe, and took some photos. In the coroner's mind, Khafre was just another black body, victimized by black-on-black violence. He whistled the tune of The All-American Rejects' "Dirty Little Secrets" as he pushed Khafre's body into the freezer. He then removed his gloves, trashed them, and turned to leave, when he heard banging and a disturbing clamor coming from the freezer. Cautiously, he made his way over to the freezer that the noise was coming from and pulled it open.

"Aahhhhh!" Khafre screamed, flailing his arms about, not knowing where he was and why.

"Good God!" yelled the coroner, running for the door.

Khufu

CHAPTER 32
SAVE HIM IN THE NEXT ONE
Three years later…

Machi sat contentedly in his new Benz, dipped in a white bathing Ape, Ape Head Sweat suit, and some while Oreo Air Jordan 4 Retros. He was on the phone pleading his case to Crystal for "accidentally" sticking his dick in her best friend Tweet. Crystal had forgiven him and agreed to rebuild their friendship, but nothing more.

Business had been lucrative for Machi and Hezron since flipping the fentanyl. They had gone behind Khafre's back and plugged themselves in with Jarrod. Hezron was relaxed in the passenger seat in a Moncler Sweat Suit and a pair of Fendi Hi-top sneakers. He scrolled on Facebook, looking for a thot to trick with, since sex with Amber was getting predictable. He took another pull from his blunt of cheese and passed it to Doughboy, who was in the back, scrolling on Facebook also. Doughboy was a chico off of Boston Avenue who met Hezron through Amber. He was a certified killer, and proficient hustler of X pills.

"Damn, my nigga, I was wondering when you was gon' pass that shit," Doughboy clowned, taking a pull from the blunt.

"I told you, roll ya own shit, lazy-ass nigga!" Hezron retorted.

"I'm finna do just that right after I smoke yo' shit!"

"You got a real nigga fucked up!" Hezron stated turning around to reach for his blunt.

Doughboy pushed his hand away. "Chill out, nigga, you know I'm just fuckin' wit'cha," Doughboy replied, laughing.

"Betta find ya ass somethin' safe to do, nigga."

"Aye! Man, I'm trying to use the fuckin' phone! Both of you niggas get the fuck out! Y'all food should be done by now, shit!" Machi was agitated.

"Nigga, I'll go right in yo' shit," Hezron muttered, getting out of the car and heading into Chucky Ducky's. Doughboy laughed before following behind Hezron.

"Who is you yellin' at?" Crystal questioned.

"My dumb-ass brother and his friend, but fuck all that. What's up wit' me pulling up on you?"

"I'm not ready for all that. Machi, you really hurt me," Crystal expressed.

"I understand that. That's why I'm trying to make it right," Machi proclaimed, letting his seat back to get more comfortable.

"I just need more time," Crystal expressed, voice saturated in pain.

"More time? It's been three years, ma!" Machi cried, lifting up to adjust the AC. As soon as he touched the knob, he saw two hooded figures coming from both directions.

"Shit!"

Boc! Boc! Boc! Boc!

Both figures made their way in front of Machi's car, blasting off shots at him as he sat helpless. They ran behind Chucky Ducky's, hopped in their getaway car and slipped away.

"Machi! Machi!" Crystal yelled frantically, trying to get a response.

Moments later, Hezron and Doughboy ran out of Chucky's with pistols out, but they were a few seconds late. The assailants were long gone.

"Brah!" Hezron yelled, opening the door. "Fuck!" Hezron panicked when he saw Machi clutching his chest.

"Nigga! Help me, put 'em in the back seat! Fuck you just standin' there for?" Doughboy snapped.

Hezron snapped out of it and helped put Machi in the back seat. Hezron got in the back seat with Machi while Doughboy hopped in the front seat and punched it to Lawnwood Medical.

"God, please! If you can't save him in this life, save him in the next one!" cried Hezron.

***

Cowboy and Smash pulled into Reno's Hotel on 21st Street and parked the whip that they rented from a smoker, for a few stones off crack. They then hopped into Cowboy's Dodge Ram and got in the wind.

"Damn, that shit was poetic!" Cowboy proclaimed excitedly, sparking a blunt.

"Made a movie out his ass," Smash added, sparking a cigarette.

"You think we got 'em?" asked Cowboy.

"Shit... If we didn't, he ain't happy. That nigga gon' lose a lung or get a shit bag or somethin' with all that lead we put in the front of that windshield." Smash laughed as he replayed how frantically Machi was moving around in the car when they were shooting.

"You a li'l wild nigga, fa real. I fucks wit'chu," Cowboy stated, handing Smash the blunt. Smash was a young wild nigga from Project Clique Gangstaz dubbed (V-Side) Vietnam. Khafre had plugged Smash with Cowboy through Lexus. Khafre was somewhere ducked off and needed a few good men to move around for him until he re-surfaced. Cowboy had proven his loyalty by moving all eighteen bricks of fentanyl that Khafre fronted on consignment. Khafre plugged Smash with Cowboy to show him how to navigate through the city of Fort Pierre. His orders were to kill everything associated with Machi and Hezron. Cowboy vowed to execute his orders.

"What the next move is?" questioned Smash.

"I'm finna drop you off and get on the road, baby boy."

"Where?"

"Seffner."

"Fuck is that?"

"Out in the country."

"Shid, I ain't doing shit. Let me slide wit'chu."

"Fuck it, shid. I ain't doin no trippin'. We gone," Cowboy asserted pulling out his phone as he headed towards I-4. He dialed a number and waited on the receiver to pick up. They answered on the third ring.

"Yeah?"

"Man down," Cowboy stated.

"Permanently?"

"Give it a few hours. We'll know then," Cowboy assured.
"Don't call me until everything is dead!"
"Say no more," replied Cowboy.
Click!

CHAPTER 33
FUCK YOU

Khafre hung up the phone and laid back as his physical therapist helped him stretch his legs out. After taking a bullet to the head, Khafre had fallen into a vegetable-like state that most people don't come back from. The fact that the coroner pronounced him dead and he somehow was revived after being stuck in the freezer brought a lot of attention Khafre's way. He was mentioned on every news channel and every talk show wanted to pick his brain and this experience. To escape the madness, Wholly took Khafre and his mother out to Atlanta and ducked them off in a mansion in Fayetteville. He had to learn how to talk and walk all over again. With the help of his mother, he became familiar with faces and what had taken place before his vegetative state. His physical therapist was a Haitian beauty from Atlanta. She was physically attracted to Khafre and was astounded at how fast he recovered.

"Khafre, I see that you have been making progress very rapidly. You're almost back to 100 percent. How do you feel about that?" Quen asked, now massaging Khafre's thighs.

"Well, I'm not the type of nigga to just lay down and wallow in the unfortunate I'm built different. But to answer your question, I feel virile, yet virulent."

"Okay, so you're vigorous and full of hate?"

"Vengeful," Khafre added, looking Quen in her beautiful calmative eyes.

"After going through what you've been through, I can understand that," Quen stated, moving her hand further up Khafre's thighs. "But before you just dive back into the belly of the beast, you should learn to enjoy what's in front of you."

Khafre smiled. "And what is that?"

Quen slipped her hand in Khafre's gym shorts and pulled his dick out.

"You know, it ain't no coming back from this, right?"

"Tell me about, it," Quen retorted, putting the head of Khafre's dick in her mouth.

The warmth from her mouth sent chills throughout Khafre's body. "Sss...damn!" Khafre cried, on the verge of cumming in Quen's mouth.

Quen pulled Khafre's dick out of her mouth, climbed on top of him, pulled her lace panties to the side. and slipped Khafre's dick into her wetness.

"Oowwww...shit!" moaned Quen as she lifted up and down, rocked back and forth, then began to grind and wind on Khafre's dick like a dancehall Queen of Jamaica.

Khafre gripped both of her pillow-soft ass cheeks and grinded with her, pushing deeper in her with each grind.

"That's it, put that pussy on me!" Khafre encouraged as he began to lift Quen up and slam her back down on his dick punitively.

"Oh fuck! Yesss, daddy, fuck me hard!" Quen cried as her ass bounced and clapped perpetually to a detectable rhythm.

"Give me that pussy!" Khafre taunted through clenched teeth.

"Oooww, fuck, I'm coming, daddy, yesss!" Quen slowed her pace, trying to catch her breath.

Out of nowhere Khafre flipped Quen on her back, put her knees next to her ears, and began to long stroke her violently with no compassion. "Take this dick!"

"Sss! Fuck! Right there daddy! Don't stop!" Quen came again and shook. "Sss. Ooow, wait! Sss! Wait!" pleaded Quen.

Khafre ignored Quen and gave her everything he had until he came.

"Aaaahhh. Shit! Fuck! My leg!" yelled Khafre as he clutched his leg, trying to massage the Charlie horse out.

Quen put her hand over her mouth and laughed. "I told yo' horny ass to stop. That's good for yo' ass," Quen pronounced, wiping the sweat from Khafre's face.

"Fuck you," Khafre stated.

"You just did." Quen smiled and then kissed Khafre on the lips.

CHAPTER 34
ANOTHER ONE

Hezron had just left Machi's bed side at Lawnwood Medical Center. The sight of his brother with tubes in his face and IVs in his arms made him feel futile. He didn't see who attempted murder on his blood, but he felt within his every fiber that Khafre was behind it. Hezron was combing through the city meticulously looking for anybody that knew Khafre or anyone who ever had a problem with his brother. He just wanted to kill for therapy.

"My fuckin' brother laid up in there wit' four holes in him and shit. He got a fuckin' collapsed lung and shit hooked up to a fuckin' breathing machine," Hezron vented as tears fell from the wells of his eyes.

"Don't trip, my nigga, we gon' put dirt on them niggas' chest first appearance, homie," Doughboy assured, passing Hezron a blunt.

"I know Khafre had something to do with this shit." Hezron took a pull from the blunt.

"I'on know, homie. I heard that nigga was a vegetable."

"It's been like, three years doe. Ain't nobody seen him. I'm tellin' you, that nigga vicious. He prolly ducked off playing puppet master and shit," replied Hezron, passing the blunt back to Doughboy.

"That nigga ducked off cuz he still a vegetable. But, if you really feel like he orchestrated that play, we'll catch 'em when he surfaces," Doughboy enunciated, passing Hezron an X pill.

"I'on pop them shit, brah."

"Just take off wit' me one time, fam. This shit gon' ease you and have you jiggin' the greatest." Doughboy popped one himself. "Come on, fam." Hezron took the pill from Doughboy's hand. "Make sho' you chew it first, brah. That bitch gon' kick in faster."

Hezron threw the pill in his mouth and chewed it up before swallowing it. "Fuck! Nigga, that shit nasty!" Hezron chased the pill down with orange juice.

"That's how you know they potent," Doughboy added, smiling.

Five minutes later, Hezron started feeling the full effect of the X. He was gritting his teeth and gripped the steering wheel tightly.

"You a'ight, fam?"

"Hell yeah, nigga, I'm good. You a'ight?" Hezron inhaled and exhaled in euphoria.

"I'm good, brah."

"Shid, I'm good, you good, bitch, we good," said Hezron, rubbing on his thigh, not really knowing how to contain his blissful high.

"Bitch, I told you that shit was gon' ease your mind."

Hezron continued to rub on his thighs as he made a left on 23rd and Canal. He drew his pistol from his right pocket swiftly and pulled into the second house on the left that belonged to Dred.

"What up, fam?" Doughboy questioned, pulling his pistol off instinct.

"I see somethin'," retorted Hezron, hopping out of his Jeep Wagoneer. A Jamaica that Hezron knew was placing a bag in a dude's hand by the name of Junebug.

"Don't shoot me!" pleaded Dred.

Junebug turned to see what Dred was pleading about. Doughboy hopped out behind Hezron.

"Wassup na, nigga?"

Boc!

The first shot hit Junebug in the shoulder, causing him to spin around and take off running. Hezron was heavy on Junebug's trail as he rounded the back of Dred's apartment.

Boc!

Another shot hit Junebug in the back, dropping him under a mango tree. The chickens and roosters that loitered in Dred's yard scattered about as Hezron and Doughboy stood over Junebug and executed him. When they came from the back of the apartment, Dred was still baffled.

"Dred, you ain't seen shit, right?" Hezron asked through clenched teeth.

"Me not see, blood clot, nothing. Me not inform, informer for dead!"

"Keep it that way," Hezron threatened, hopping back in his whip with Doughboy behind him.

"Why you let 'em live, fam?" asked Doughboy.

"He's a friend of my father."

"Why we killed the other nigga?"

Hezron pulled off, feeling more galvanized after the kill. "That bitch-ass nigga owes my brother twenty dollars."

"Twenty dollars?" questioned Doughboy.

"Yeah, nigga. Twenty! Give me another pill," said Hezron.

Khufu

CHAPTER 35
FUCK!

Cowboy got off an I-4 and entered into Seffner, his hometown, "The Kuntree." It was a small, populated town where everybody knows everybody. Cowboy and his little circle were known for getting crack money, but once Khafre put fentanyl in his possession, it spread through The Kuntree like wildfire. He headed straight to Pine Street to check on a trap spot he'd placed his cousin 's name.

"Damn, my nigga! This shit look like some real backwoods redneck type. Shit! The fuck you got a nigga at?" Smash asked, unimpressed. Cowboy laughed.

"Relax, baby boy. It's a lot of money down here." Cowboy stated, pulling in the trap spot.

"Well, let's get it and go. I ain't feelin' this shit."

"Listen. We just put holes in a nigga on front street. We gotta lay low, baby boy."

"Ain't nobody see us. Even if they did, they know how I'm comin'."

"I hear all that, but let's just stay down here tonight, and see what the news and Facebook talkin' 'bout. I'll take you back tomorrow."

Smash exhaled, agitated. "Fuck it, man."

"Get out, let me introduce you to my people." Cowboy got out with Smash following behind him. Instead of knocking on the door, Cowboy just entered the apartment.

Dontae was in the living room smoking weed with a table full of X pills and four white girls surrounding him.

"Wassup, Cuz?" Cowboy greeted. "This my li'l homie, Smash. He from Fort Pierce."

"Fort Pierce, huh? What do they call that shit? Umm...Killa Kounty?"

"You better know it!" Smash retorted arrogantly.

Dontae chuckled. "Okay, Smash. I'm Dontae. You see anything in here you like, just help yaself."

"Respect," Smash replied.

"Aye, let me holla at'chu right quick, fam," Cowboy asked Dontae, then headed in the back room.

"Excuse me ladies, I'll be back in a few. Smash make yourself at home." Dontae headed in the back room. As soon as he entered, Cowboy got straight to the point.

"Wassup, Cuz, you got my money?"

"What kind of stupid-ass question is that?" Dontae asked, offended.

"One that requires an answer," Cowboy shot back brisky.

"You know I got it."

"Okay, let's see it. You got a house full of white hoes. I need to know that you ain't trickin' off my profit."

Dontae went into a closet and pulled out a cache. "Here, nigga! Don't never disrespect my hustle. The nigga you need to be checking is Nate."

"Nate? For what? Nate is a loyal nigga."

Dontae laughed. "Nate been round here draggin' your name through the mud."

"Not Nate!"

"He says ever since you've been going to Fort Pierce, you've been changing. He say you think you are above everybody, cuz you found a plugman. He say he ain't paying you shit!"

"Let me know when you're done," said Cowboy in disbelief.

"I ain't shittin' you, Cuz, you'll see for yourself," Dontae assured him.

Cowboy left out of the room and saw that Smash was enjoying himself. "I'ma need you to wrap that shit up. We got bidness to handle," he said.

"What bidness I got down here? You go ahead. I'll be here when you get back." Smash laid his head back on the sofa and continued to enjoy getting his dick sucked.

Cowboy walked over to where Smash was, grabbed both snow bunnies by their hair, and pulled them off of Smash.

"Brah, what type of time you on?" asked Smash, face hard as granite.

"Bidness before pleasure, baby boy. Get'cha shit back in ya pants. Let's roll," Cowboy ordered, then walked off.

"Excuse me, ladies." Smash got himself together, then stood to leave. "You stopped me from getting my dick sucked. I better get to kill a bitch behind this shit!" yelled Smash. "So, what's up? What bidness we got so important that you had to stop me from getting groovy wit' dem pink toes?" Smash asked smugly.

"We gotta li'l situation over here on Parsons and Calhoun Street."

"What that gotta do wit' me?" questioned Smash, lighting a cigarette.

"We do bidness, for the same nigga?"

"I'm listening."

"Okay, it's a nigga over here, playin wit' our paper. He my li'l partner, but if he cross me, he gets it."

"You'll kill ya partner 'bout a li'l paper?" Smash asked with a smile on his face.

"Give his family something to do," Cowboy proclaimed with no empathy.

"Slime life, huh?" clowned smash.

"Nall, real life," Cowboy replied, pulling in a field that had only one trailer in the middle of it. "Come on," muttered Cowboy, hopping out of his truck.

Smash followed suit.

When Cowboy approached the door to the trailer, he could hear the sounds of Young Boy Never Broke Again "Know Like I Know" blaring from Nate's speakers. Cowboy opened the door and entered with Smash behind him. Nate never heard them enter because of the music and did not see them because he had his face buried in a plate of coke. Cowboy turned the music down, causing Nate to look up.

"I see you enjoying the fruits of my labor," Cowboy stated, voice thickening with menace as he stood in front of Nate.

"Yo 'labor?" Nate implored, wiping coke residue from his nose. "Nigga, I'm the one movin the pack while you taking vacations and shit"

"First off, lower yo' fuckin voice. Secondly, if you movin' the pack, where the fuck my money?"

"You get it when you get it, nigga! And why would I have to lower my tone? This my mothafuckin' spot! And who the fuck is this off brand-ass nigga you done brought in my shit?"

Smash smirked wickedly, showing all sixteen gold teeth. He was only seventeen, midnight black with a bald head. Most people found him threatening, but the coke put a battery pack in Nate, blinding him to the fact that Smash was a young contract killa.

"Nigga, I'm the one who put chu in this mothafucka! You know what?" Cowboy slapped the plate of coke on the floor. "Go get my fuckin' money! Right now!" yelled Cowboy.

Nate looked at his half ounce of coke sprawled all over the floor, then back at Cowboy with blood in his eyes. He reached under his little table, grabbed a snub nose .38 revolver, stood, and pointed it at Cowboy's face.

"Why the fuck you did that? Huh? You gon' fuckin' pay for my shit, nigga!"

Boc! Boc!

Smash hit Nate in his head and chest. His body hit the couch, then rolled on the floor in between the table and couch.

"Fuck! This stupid-ass nigga done got his ass killed. Fuck it, is what it is. Help me search the spot. Before we leave, we burn this bitch to the ground," pronounced Cowboy.

"Alright," Smash replied emotionlessly.

CHAPTER 36
WOO

It was a beautiful night in downtown Atlanta. The stars were out, the breeze was balmy, and the women were beyond gorgeous. Quen had offered to take Khafre somewhere to ease his mind. She chose to take him to the Sundial restaurant, where the top of the building rotates while you enjoy your meal and the view of Downtown Atlanta. Quen enjoyed a nice steak with garlic noodles, while Khafre dined on a Vegan salad. During recovery, Khafre read a lot of health books and became a vegan once informed on what meat and dairy products do to the body. Knowing that a no-flesh diet enables the body to heal itself, Khafre opted to be a vegan for life.

"You sure you don't want some grilled chicken with that salad?" Quen teased before placing a piece of steak in her mouth.

"You know better than that .I'm on my Dr. Sebi flex," affirmed Khafre.

"Dr. Sebi, huh?" Quen asked sardonically. "I don't mean to be brash, but my grandmother lived to be ninety-one years old. She ate plenty of pork and dairy products."

"Imagine if she didn't. She could have lived to be one 110."

Quen chuckled, then took a sip from her wine glass.

"No disrespect to your grandmother, but in a sense, we are what we eat. When you eat right, it puts the spirit in a state of nirvana and allows you to vibrate on a higher frequency than flesh eaters. See how low your vibration is right now? It's cuz you shoveling that carcass in yo' face like a true savage," Khafre clowned attempting to grab Quen's plate.

"Boy, stop, before I cut chu," retorted Quen, pulling her plate closer to her. "And you a trip. My vibrations are just fine. You ain't say that, when I was vibrating on that thang," said Quen, smiling before placing another piece of steak in her mouth.

"You was vibratin' so good, I thought you had Parkinson's," Khafre joked, laughing for the first time since being shot.

Quen laughed and hit Khafre playfully on the arm. "You so silly," proclaimed Quen, leaning in and kissing Khafre passionately.

Khafre obliged, reaching his hand under Quen's dress, when his phone rang. He broke away from Quen's luscious succulent lips and answered his phone. "Yeah, what up?"

"I'm headed back to the city," Cowboy informed.

"A'ight. What's the update on that demo?"

"They say it's a fifty-fifty chance."

"Fifty-fifty, huh?"

"Yeah," Cowboy replied dryly.

"You a animal?"

"Pure breed."

"Then I shouldn't have to tell you to touch everything he love! You need me to do a walk through?'

"Nall, stay where you are. I got it," Cowboy assured.

"A'ight. I done told you, don't call me till it's dirt on a nigga chest." Khafre hung up on Cowboy.

Quen gave Khafre a sullen look. "Why are you talking like that over the phone? You know better than that," voiced Quen.

"You right. I tripped out. That's why I need you to stick around. Only you can calm the savage beast."

"You want me to stick around, huh?" Quen smiled.

"Undoubtedly," Khafre replied.

"You're so goofy. I'll see what I can do."

"Fair enough." Quen gazed at Khafre concernedly. "What up, ma?"

"Khafre, what are your religious beliefs?"

"I'm not a religious type of nigga. I focus on the interior rather than exterior, preferably."

"How do you mean?" questioned Quen curiously.

"Instead of searching and looking for some shit outside myself to save me, I search within. I believe in me."

"So, you're spiritual? I wanna take you to see some people for protection."

"So, you wanna take me to get woo on me?"

"Protection, yes."

"I ain't got nothing against it, cuz my ancestor operated with it, but I'm good. I stay strapped. I'on need that shit."

"You was strapped last time you got shot. Don't be stubborn. Let me help you," Quen offered.

Khafre thought it over for a moment. "Don't that shit be back-firing?"

"If you don't abide by what's asked of you, then yes," Quen admitted truthfully.

Khafre could sense that Quan cared for his well-being. He grabbed both of her hands and placed a gentle kiss upon them.

"Let's do it," Khafre stated.

Quen smiled, then placed another kiss on Khafre's lips. "It's one more thing I forgot to tell you."

"What's that?"

"We gotta go to Haiti."

Khufu

CHAPTER 37
STUPID NIGGA

It was a bright, sultry day in the projects. The kids played jovially, wetting each other with water hoses, while their parents basked in the shade on their porches. Hezron was flipping the meat on the grill while Doughboy sat on the porch next to Amber and her little girl Hezy. Amber and Hezron now had a one-year-old daughter together, whom Hezron adored. He offered to take Amber out of the projects, but she was adamant about staying. Hezron had his own place aside from his father's, but he came by every day to make sure Amber and his daughter were straight.

"That food ain't done yet? Damn!" whined Amber, drained from the heat wave.

"That Remy eatin' the linin' out'cha stomach, huh? This what happens when you wake up at eight in the morning sippin' straight liquor. Sit yo' ass down till this shit done!" Hezron retorted.

"Nigga, whatever! Watch Hezy.

Hezron had to close the grill to tend to his daughter. He picked her up out of her walker and placed kisses on her soft cheeks. "That's Daddy's baby," said Hezron, lifting Hezy in the air. Hezy smiled at her father and drooled on his face. "Damn, Hezy!" proclaimed Hezron, placing Hezy back in her baby walker and wiping his face.

Doughboy laughed and passed Hezron the blunt.

"Ain't shit funny, nigga."

"It is to me," Doughboy replied, taking a sip from his Corona.

"We gon' see, how funny shit is when yo' ass don't get shit off this grill.'

"You got me, fucked up, homie. I went half on that meat."

"What I care 'bout that?"

"Whateva, nigga." Hezron passed the blunt back to Doughboy. "Aye, watch Hezy while I run inside real quick."

"That's my goddaughter, you know she's straight wit' me."

"A'ight."

Hezron went inside to check on Amber. When he entered the hallway, he could hear a sniffing sound coming from the bathroom. He placed his ear to the door, and heard it again. Amber forgot to lock the door. Hezron turned the knob and opened it. Amber didn't even flinch or tense up when she saw Hezron. She courageously navigated the key that had nearly a half of gram on it to her nose and inhaled.

"Damn, you can't fuckin knock? A bitch can't have any type of privacy round this motherfucka?" Amber ranted, wiping the coke residue from her nose.

"Bitch! You a fuckin' coke head now?" questioned Hezron as his blood began to boil.

"And? Nigga, you pop pills and shit! What'chu, ain't think I knew?" snapped Amber, filling the key with coke again and bringing it to her nose.

Smack! Hezron slapped the shit out of Amber, causing coke to fly about, as she fell from the toilet onto the floor. He pulled his pistol swiftly from his Balmain jeans and hit Amber across the head with it.

"Aaahhh!" screamed Amber, grabbing her head and balling up.

"Don't scream now, bitch!" Hezron kicked Amber in her stomach, knocking the wind out of her. "So this where all my fuckin' money going, huh? You like to treat cha nose, huh?" Hezron squatted next to Amber, grabbed her by her hair, and stuck his pistol in her mouth. "Bitch! I should blow yo' fuckin' head off!" Hezron stated through clenched teeth.

"Brah! Don't do it, homie! Think about'cha daughter," advised Doughboy.

Hezron turned to look behind him and saw Doughboy holding his daughter.

"Come on, homie. She ain't worth it. Come back outside wit'cha daughter."

Hezron looked at Amber, then at his daughter. "You right. She ain't worth it." Hezron grilled Amber before grabbing his daughter and walking out. Once outside, Hezron kissed his daughter, then placed her back in her baby walker.

"I'on know what happened, homie, but I'm glad you didn't blow her head off. You got a, daughter to look after, homie."

"Yeah, you right. This bitch in there snortin' and shit" Hezron walked over to the grill to check the meat.

"Damn. That's a hard vice to shake," added Doughboy, shaking his head. He put a blunt in his mouth and sparked it.

Boc! Boc! Boc!

Out of instinct, Hezron ducked behind the barbeque grill and snatched out his FNH .40 Hezron returned fire, putting holes in the rust-colored Crown Vic door. Doughboy had grabbed cover behind a concrete trestle, pulled his two-twin SIG .40's, and came from behind the trestle, letting both pistols go, causing the Crown Vic to swerve onto the curb, but it still managed to get away. When Doughboy turned around with the pistols in hand, he saw Hezron on his knees, cradling his daughter with tears in his eyes as blood seeped through his fingers and dropped down his forearm.

"Oh shit!" cried Doughboy, placing both hands on his head with the pistols still in them.

Hezron's whole body was trembling when Amber walked out of her apartment and saw her daughter in Hezron's arms.

"Whose blood is that?" Amber asked hysterically, rushing over to grab Hezy out of Hezron's arms. Once she had Hezy in her arms, she saw that the blood was, in fact, Hezy's and that there was no life left in her. Amber wailed in agony, while Hezron was in a state of shock. Doughboy pulled out his phone and called an ambulance.

"This is all yo' fuckin' fault! You got our daughter killed, you stupid-ass nigga! I fuckin hate chu!"

***

Even though there was no life left in Hezy, Amber, Hezron, and Doughboy waited in the emergency lobby, hoping and praying for an act of God. The news had spread rapidly on social media, which prompted Crystal to pull up and be by Amber's side. Being a mother herself, she sympathized with Amber's loss, but couldn't remotely begin to fathom losing her daughter. Not having any words of comfort, all Crystal could do was rub Amber's back as she held her face in her palms and wept uncontrollably. Doughboy was posted against a wall with one foot up and his head to the sky while Hezron paced back and forth with a blood-saturated shirt when the doctor came out to deliver the update on Hezy.

"Ms. Smith?"

"Yes?" Amber stood to face the doctor with tears in her eyes.

"Your daughter didn't make it. I'm sorry." The doctor turned to leave as quick as he came.

Hezron fell to his knees and placed his forehead on the floor as if he was a Muslim making salat.

"Ahhhh!" Amber screamed as she rushes over to Hezron and kicked him in the face, busting his nose.

Doughboy quickly grabbed Amber and attempted to calm her down. "Chill out!" yelled Doughboy. "Just chill. We gon' get the niggas who did it! I promise!" Doughboy assured.

Amber just fell to the floor and wept.

"Make sure she, okay, alright? I gotta go," Crystal stated, heading towards the elevator.

Once on the elevator, she went up to the third floor and headed to room 305. When she entered the room, she was confounded to see Tweet sitting by Machi's bedside. Tweet turned and locked eyes with Crystal. The resentment on Crystal's face showed. She wanted to crush Tweet again, but instead, she turned to leave the room. Tweet followed behind her.

"Crystal, I'm sorry!" yelled Tweet as she caught up to Crystal.

Crystal stopped and turned to face Tweet, her face still tight with emotions.

"Shh! Please keep it down," a nurse walking by muttered.

"This a hospital, not no damn library, bitch, fuck you!" replied Tweet, causing Crystal to laugh momentarily. "Oooww, I made you laugh, bitch. I know you forgive me."

"I'on know about all that," Crystal replied, wiping the smile from her face.

"How the hell you don't know, and I forgave yo' ass for hitting me upside my damn head wit' a pistol?"

Crystal laughed again.

"Bitch, that shit is not funny. I still got knots on my shit, hoe. Feel what'chu did to my shit." Tweet grabbed Crystal's hand, but Crystal snatched it away.

"Girl, lower your damn voice, 'fore you get me locked up in here."

"I will, if you forgive me."

"I gotta think about that shit."

"You really gon' switch up on me over some dick?"

"You know I was feelin' him."

"I understand that, and I'm sorry. But I ain't put no gun to his head. He climbed in this pussy on his own."

Crystal thought about Tweet's words. "You right. I accept that, and I accept your apology.

Tweet smiled and hugged Crystal's neck.

"Bitch, I missed yo' ass!" Tweet exclaimed excitedly.

"I ain't gon' lie, I missed you too. So, how Machi in there doing?"

"He gone be a'ight. He opened his eyes, but he went right back to sleep. They keepin' him heavily sedated. He hasn't spoken a word either. You know one of the bullets hit him in the neck and he got a collapsed lung. He lucky to be alive.

"Damn, I was just downstairs with Amber,"

"What happened to Amber?"

"Her daughter got killed in a drive by."

Tweet put a hand over her mouth as tear fell from her right eye.

Khufu

CHAPTER 38
WHAT WE DOIN'?

"Chris, let me get a blow," Amber begged for the third time.

Chris was the owner of a pool hall on 11th Street. Everybody hung out at the pool hall after hours looking for dope or sex. The club had just let out, so there was a nice crowd out.

"Bitch! Get the fuck from outta my establishment, asking for dope and shit," demanded Chris.

"Awl, nigga! Don't act like you don't snort. I know you got some. Sell me a gram.

"I'ma call the police on yo' ass, hoe! Get the fuck out!"

"Damn, nigga! You playin' police games now? What type of time, you on?"

"Fuck all that, hoe. Get the fuck out my shit!"

"What'chu want, some pussy?" Amber asked, pulling the tight panties out of her pussy and standing bowlegged.

"Naw, that pussy got too many bodies on it, I'm good. Get out!"

Before Amber could continue to bargain, she felt someone grab her hand.

"Come on, I got'chu."

Amber looked up and saw a familiar face lurking up under a Moncler hoodie. With no words, Amber let the familiar-looking man guide her outside of the pool hall.

"You way too gorgeous, to play yo' self like that, ma," said the man with the familiar face.

"Don't I know you?" questioned Amber.

"Nall, ma, I ain't even from around here.

"I know you from somewhere."

"Look, ma, you got a whip?"

"Yeah, why? What'chu want tonight?" Amber bit her bottom lip, then grabbed a handful of the man's dick before leading him to her 2022 Altima. Once inside, the unknown man let his seat back, then sent a message from his phone.

"Who you texting?" questioned Amber, sliding her hand down his pants as she drove.

"Pay attention to what's in front of you, ma."

"That's exactly what I'm doin'," retorted Amber, removing her hand and sucking her finger

"It's like that?"

"You finna find out," boasted Amber.

The strange man chuckled.

Five minutes later, Amber pulled in front of her apartment in the projects and cut her car off.

"Let me ask you something."

"You can ask me whatever," replied Amber

"As pretty as you are, why you snortin' dope? Why you out here like this?"

Amber's mood changed as she lowered her head before replying. "I just lost my daughter in a drive-by. I'm dealing with a lot right now. So, this is how I cope with it. It's really my stupid-ass baby daddy fault."

"Whatcha mean? Where he at now?"

"Prolly somewhere looking for their ass. I'on wanna talk about him. What we doin'?" Amber asked, sticking her hand back in his pants.

Moments later, a truck pulled behind Amber's car.

"Check this out, ma. I gotta get in the wind." He went to his pocket and handed Amber a gram. "Snortin this shit ain't gon' bring yo' daughter back." He got out of the car, hopped in the truck that pulled up, and pulled off.

"Oh well," muttered Amber. She took a bump and thought to herself, *Damn, that nigga look just like Khafre.*

***

Hezron and Doughboy were combing through the streets looking for the nigga responsible for his daughter's death. The only problem was, they were chasing a ghost. As soon as they agreed to turn in for the night, Hezron got a call from Jarrod to pick up a load. After picking the load up, they put it in a stash house and headed to Amber's apartment to cool it until something came up.

"So, what's good, homie? We gon' wait till we get our man before we move this work? Or are we just out here?" asked Doughboy, lighting a blunt.

"Give it a few days, then we go open up shop," Hezron retorted, pulling in next to Amber's Altima.

"I'on think that's a good idea homie. War and money don't mix. We gotta kill these niggas first," declared Doughboy, passing the blunt to Hezron.

"We gon' get 'em in due time, but this money gotta be made," affirmed Hezron getting out of his whip with Doughboy behind him.

"Look at that. Stupid-ass bitch, done fell asleep in the car." Hezron knocked on the driver's window. "Bitch, get'cha stupid ass up and go in the house!" yelled Hezron

"Calm down, homie," advised Doughboy, understanding Amber's pain of losing her daughter

"Fuck her!"

Hezron opened the door and saw Amber laid back in her seat with her head back and blood coming from her nose. "Amber!" yelled Hezron shaking her. Amber didn't show signs of life, so Hezron checked for a pulse. There wasn't one.

Amber thought she was sniffing coke, but she was given Fentanyl.

Khufu

CHAPTER 39
OGUN

It was a beautiful day to be at sea. The sun was beaming, and the ocean was multi-colored and not as rough as usual. The drinks were flowing and the two women that Jarrod had on board were extremely breathtaking. It had been a good year for Jarrod. He'd made millions of dollars from Fentanyl distribution, and looked forward to many more fruitful expenditures.

Boc! Boc!

Jarrod was in the cockpit when he heard gunshots coming from the wheel house. He reached under the cushion on his sofa, grabbed a .44 magnum Anaconda, and told the women to stay down. When he made it to the wheel house, he discovered the captain with a hole in his head, sprawled out on the floor.

"Jarrod, what the lick read?"

Jarrod spun and lined the perpetrator up in the sights of his Magnum. "Khafre?'" asked Jarrod, confused as ever.

"In the flesh," Khafre retorted.

"How the fuck did you get on my yacht?" Jarrod snarled, still aiming his pistol at Khafre face.

"That's neither here nor there."

"The hell it ain't!"

"Recognize what's in yo' sight, and that which is hidden from you will become plain to you."

"What?"

"There is nothing hidden which will not become manifested."

"Dude! Kill the enigma, I got a fuckin' gun in your face!"

"You betrayed me," Khafre asserted in a dangerously calm tone.

"What'chu speaking on?"

"You went behind my back and did bidness wit' my people."

"I thought you were a vegetable. It's just business."

"Man must learn to increase his sense of responsibility and the fact that everything he does, will have its consequences," Khafre philosophized as he inched towards Jarrod's trembling hand.

Jarrod squeezed the trigger seven times, but it didn't fire. He'd just loaded it when he boarded the yacht. He was a bit befuddled as to why his brand-new gun didn't fire. Jarrod checked to see if it was loaded, and it was.

Khafre smiled wickedly. "I'm covered by LWA!"

"What?"

"Ogun!"

BOC! BOC! BOC! BOC!

Khafre lifted his nighthawk 10mm and planted three holes in Jarrod's chest. After killing both women on board, he dragged all four bodies to the stern and threw them overboard. He then took one of Jarrod's jet skis and rode into shore.

CHAPTER 40
DO YOU

It was a dispirited day in Fort Pierce, Florida. Since Amber and Hezy's deaths were so close in tandem, Hezron decided to have a joint funeral and bury them side by side. Everybody knew Amber, but the death of Hezy brought the whole city out, old and young. After the funeral, Hezron had arranged for white horses and carriages to carry Amber and Hezy's Dior caskets through the city one last time. A parade of women and children marched behind them, and all the major dope boys followed behind the women and children in their tricked-out whips.

Khafre trailed Hezron's Mercedes G63 in his heavily-tinted Camaro. He could have easily pulled alongside of Hezron and Swiss cheesed his vehicle with the M10 on his passenger seat holding a box clip that contained two hundred and fifty rounds, but decided against it due to the children. He also knew that Hezron couldn't pinpoint who was really giving him pressure on every corner. He could toy with Hezron until he decided to kill him.

While in thought, Khafre's phone rang. "What's up?" answered Khafre.

"Hey baby. I'm callin' to check on you," Quen stated.

"I'm good. How are you?"

"I'm fine. I took your mother out to eat."

"That's what's up."

"So, when are you coming back?"

"When it's over."

"Well, you need to hurry up, I'm missing you like crazy!" cried Quen.

"Won't be long."

"Okay, I love you."

"I hear you."

"Oh, you can't tell me, you love me?"

"Have I ever?"

"No but'cha know you do."

"Listen, I'm on one right now, call me back, ma."

175

"Hold up, yo' mother wanna talk to you," Quen said, handing Shantell the phone.

"Khafre?"

"Wassup, Mama?"

"Make sho' you make it back to me. You hear me?"

"Act like you know who my father is," Khafre interjected arrogantly.

Shantell chuckled. "I hear you, I wanted to tell you that them twins keep calling. They say it's important"

"A'ight, Mama, I'ma get at 'em."

"I love you, boy."

"Love you too, Mama."

Khafre hung up. "I'ma see you later," Khafre muttered to himself, referring to Hezron as he turned off and headed in another direction.

***

Smash had Cowboy take them to one of his li'l strippers houses on Airport Road. Smash always used Ms. Kitty's place as a duck off spot after pulling capers. Kitty was a mulatto beauty known for getting money and having a snappa between her legs. She was a solid bitch from the hood. Already expecting Smash and Cowboy, she opened the door when they pulled up wearing next to nothing. Smash hopped out of the whip with Cowboy behind him and greeted Kitty with a hug, gripping her soft cheeks.

"Damn, a nigga miss yo' ass, like a mothafucka!" Smash stated excitedly.

"Oh yeah? What'chu miss about it?" Kitty asked Smash while eyeing Cowboy.

"Everything!"

"I hear you. Who you got wit'chu?"

"This my partna, Cowboy, the one I told you about," Smash said, walking in the house.

"What's up li'l mama?" greeted Cowboy.

"Heyyy, come on in." Kitty stepped aside and let Cowboy in. "Y'all can help yourself to some of that Henny on the table," Kitty offered.

Smash wasted no time pouring him a coup.

"I'm cool," assured, Cowboy having a seat on a butter soft sectional.

"You sho'?" Kitty lit a blunt and sat next to Cowboy.

"Yeah, thank you doe."

"You are short as hell.   What'chu like 5'4"?"

"Five-four exact."

Feeling the tension between Kitty and Cowboy, Smash intervened.

"I thought you said you had a friend fo' my homie."

Kitty chuckled furtively.

"Oh yeah," she replied, handing Cowboy the blunt. "Come on from back there!" Kitty yelled.

Smash lifted his cup to down the rest of it. When he brought the cup back down, he spit liquor on the floor. "What the fuck?" Smash muttered in shock.

"Damn, li'l homie. Our first time meeting and you spit on a nigga?"

"My bad, big homie. You startled a nigga. And what the fuck you doin' in here?"

"We'll get to that in a minute. Kitty, excuse yourself, baby girl," Khafre demanded.

Kitty got up and hugged Khafre. He gave her a forehead kiss and told her to wait on his call. Kitty then left out her house, jumped in her ride, and left.

"Khafre! What's good, how you feeling?" asked Cowboy.

"I'm feeling pretty good, how 'bout yaself?" Khafre grabbed the bottle of Henny and took a seat across from Cowboy.

"You know how this shit go." Cowboy passed the blunt to Khafre.

"Aye, Smash, come have a seat, li'l homie. Let me have a word wit'chu boys."

Smash had a seat next to Cowboy. "What's good?" Smash asked, confused as to why Khafre was there and how he knew Kitty.

"I see y'all been spinning pretty good, you know, giving niggas' families something to do."

"Yeah, we've been swinging heavy!" boasted Smash.

"So, which one of you niggas killed the newborn?"

"I'on see how that matters. You said kill everything, correct?" asked Smash, slightly aggressive.

"We kill killas, maybe a woman if need be, but babies and shit?" Khafre shook his head

"It is what it is, brah," Smash replied with an air of dismissal.

"That li'l girl was my cousin, nigga."

"Maann!" Smash drew his pistol swiftly and pointed it at Khafre. "I only did what the fuck you told me to do nigga! Fuck is wrong wit'chu?"

Khafre smirked. "Do you, li'l nigga," Khafre taunted, blowin' smoke from his nose.

Click! Smash pulled the trigger, but his gun jammed.

Boc!

Cowboy hit Smash in the side of his head, then wiped the blood splatter from his face. "Damn! I thought he hit'chu. You lucky that bitch jammed," pronounced Cowboy.

"I ain't dying no time soon."

Khafre had traveled to a place in Haiti called Uh Ba LeBe to see Quen's uncle, who was a Voodoo priest. After a blood sacrifice, he took fifteen bullets and made a potion out of the gunpowder and made Khafre drink it. He also gave Khafre a red bandana that had a knot tied at the end of it and told him to never untie it. As long as he followed the instruction of the priest, he would be protected by the LWA.

Khafre pulled his burner phone out and dialed a number.

"Yeah, who's speaking?"

"Baby Haitian, this Khafre."

"What dey do, goon? It's been a long time," Baby Haitian said excitedly.

"I'm back out'chere ya hear me."

"Talk to me."

"I got something for you."

"Drop the addy, goon.

Khufu

CHAPTER 41
SAY NO MO'

After paying Baby Haitian to clean Kitty's house and get rid of Smash's body, Khafre bent through the city behind heavy tint with Cowboy. He took him through every hood and showed him what areas to network in, and who was at war with who.

"Listen. I respect how you handled yourself back there, and how you were keeping it one-hunnid wit' my money. So far, you seem like a solid nigga," Khafre proclaimed, pulling in the back of the Brown Store on 25th Street.

"You know, I love to do good bidness. I'ma always keep it real wit' those who do the same for me. As fo' the li'l nigga Smash. I wanted to step on 'em, but didn't know how you were going to take it," Cowboy admitted.

"I can see that. Everybody know kids off limits. That nigga wasn't my people anyway. I met him through Lexus."

"Oh yeah? When was the last time you talked to her?"

"'Bout a year ago. She the one plugged me wit' Smash."

"That's crazy. But she been askin' me bout'cha and shit. She say you keep changing yo' number," said Cowboy.

"I'ma get at her when I get a moment. Check this out, doe. I'ma sho' you somethin', and I'm only showing you this cuz I trust you."

"Okay, wassup?"

"Come on." Khafre got out of the whip with Cowboy behind him.

"Where the hell you takin' me?" questioned Cowboy, following Khafre behind the Brown Store and up the stairs.

"You don't trust a nigga?"

"I do, but this shit look creepy as fuck back here," admitted Cowboy clutching on his pistol.

Khafre laughed. "Relax, homie." Khafre opened the door to his apartment on top of the Brown Store and entered. "Welcome to the spot."

When Cowboy entered the apartment, he noticed boxes every-where. "What all this? You moved back and forgot to unpack?" asked Cowboy, cloning the door behind him.

"Nall. You lookin' at fifty bales of weed. Each bale got twenty pound of loud in it. That's a thousand pounds, nigga."

"You bullshittin'. If it was a thousand pounds in here, you'd smell it.'

"This shit was wrapped up by the best. Bust one open."

Cowboy didn't hesitate to see if Khafre was bluffing. His eyes lit up when he saw the truth. "Okay, so what's next?"

"You can fuck with it?'

"Of course!"

"A'ight. Bring me a ticket."

"A million?"

"Yeah."

Cowboy did the math in his head and quickly saw that a million was only a thousand dollars a pound. He could easily move them for two-thousand and make him a million dollars too.

"I call that," retorted Cowboy.

"It's just one catch to it, doe."

"A mill ticket? Whatever it is, I'm on it!"

"Finish the job."

"What job?"

"Hezron."

Cowboy thought for a second before responding. "Say no more."

"Already."

CHAPTER 42
DUMBASS

Cowboy sat impassively in a black-on-black Gallant, across the street from Patty's Seafood Restaurant and watched Hezron interact with the owner. He had no idea that the owner was, in fact, Hezron's grandmother. As soon as he lit a cigarette, his phone rang. He started to ignore it, but saw that it was his li'l homie Dontae.

"Dontae, baby boy, you have to hit me back. I'm on something right now," Cowboy interjected briskly.

"Aye, man! When the fuck you coming back to Seffner?"

"I'm handlin' bidness, baby boy. Why wassup? Everything a'ight?'

"Did you ever go holla at Nate?"

"Nall, I didn't even waste my time. I headed straight to Fort Pierce," lied Cowboy. "Why, wassup?"

"They found him in his trailer. His shit was burned to the ground."

"You know Nate was getting high and shit. He prolly burned his house down, fuckin' off and shit."

"That could be possible. But the fact that they found a hole in his head kills all that," Dontae retorted.

"Aye, let me hit'chu back. I'm a head back to the Kuntree prolly tomorrow, we'll talk about this shit then. And I'ma have something for ya too," stated Cowboy, staying a few cars behind Hezron.

"A'ight. Make sho' you call me back, nigga!"

"Fa'sho'."

Cowboy hung up and followed Hezron to a house on Avenue S. He noticed Hezron stopping out of his Benz as if he was in a rush. Cowboy wanted to catch him off guard before he came back out, so he parked on the side of the road and hopped out in a black hoodie. He entered through two glass sliding doors and saw that the garage was fully furnished with plush sofas, flat screen TVs, and a pool table. There was a wall full of family pictures that separated the hangout area from the washer and dryer. To the left was a door that led into the kitchen. Hezron had left it open while moving too fast.

Cowboy clutched his Glock 16 and entered the kitchen with a mill ticket on his mind.

Boc!

"Stupid nigga!" pronounced Doughboy, who was already waiting behind the wall.

Hezron had peeped Cowboy at Patty's Seafood restaurant. When he saw that he was being followed, he sent a text to Doughboy to bake a cake for whoever was following him.

Hezron came out of the living room and saw Cowboy on the kitchen floor bleeding. Due to Cowboys nerves still being active, one of his legs kicked back and forth as if he was fighting to live. Hezron put two more slugs in Cowboy's head. When there was no longer a pulse, the Rolex that Cowboy was wearing stopped identifying his time of death.

"You know this nigga?" questioned Doughboy, going through Cowboys cargos.

"Nall, I'on know this nigga."

"Damn, this shit crazy, homie!" retorted Doughboy.

"Wassup?" asked a confused Hezron.

"I think this the nigga who was in the car when Hezy got killed, homie," Doughboy pronounced as his eyes grew perceptibly wider.

"Oh yeah?

"Yeah, I think it's him."

"How the fuck can you tell wit' all them holes in his head?"

"Cuz, nigga! When he was shooting, I saw the same Rollie hanging out the window."

Hezron nodded his head in agreement as he fell into a perceived state.

"You a'ight, homie?"

"Yeah."

"Well, get right. You got a whole body on Grandma's kitchen floor.'

"This nigga ain't come to rob. He came for blood, homie."

"So, what'chu sayin', homie?"

"Tell you later. Help me put this dumb-ass nigga and his whip in Taylors Creek."

CHAPTER 43
WHAT DEY DO, NIGGA?

Khafre sat in his Camaro in front of the Brown Store and dialed Cowboy's number for the fifth time. All he kept getting was the voicemail, and it had been a week since he saw him. Khafre decided to call Lexus. She picked up on the second ring.

"Who's calling?"

"This Khafre."

"Well, I'll be damned! How are you doing, stranger?"

"You know how I'm living," Khafre responded arrogantly.

"That I do. I been trying to call you, but I guess you switched digits on me."

"Yeah, this is my new math right here."

"Wassup? Swang through, let me see you."

"When I get a moment, I'ma pull up. Listen though. You ain't seen or heard from Cowboy?"

"I did, about two weeks ago. I tried to call him yesterday, but no answer. Why?"

"No pressure; I just had something for him. If he calls you, call me, ya hear me?'

"Okay. Sounds like you rushing off the phone. You don't miss me?"

"I think about'cha a li'l piece. I'ma pull up, give me a minute. I'm on something right now!"

Wholly came out of the store and tapped on the passenger door. Khafre unlocked the door and let him in.

"Okay. Don't change ya number again."

"I gotcha." Khafre hung the phone up.

"Khafre, my friend, how are you feeling?"

"I'm good, ock. How 'bout yaself?"

"Business as usual. So, how long are you in town for?"

"I'ma take a flight back to Atlanta tonight. Why? What's good, Ock?"

"Because, my friend, the longer you stay, the longer your mother worries. Make sure you make it back to her and Quen."

"Quen?"

"Yes, Quen. She already told me, buddy. She's good for you. Treat her right,"

Khafre just nodded his head, agreeing to his advice. "Listen, before I leave, I got something you might be interested in."

"What is it?"

"I got a thousand pounds of high grade weed in my apartment upstairs. You interested?"

"A thousand pounds?"

"Yeah,"

Wholly thought for a minute. "How much you asking for price?"

"I need a million."

Wholly exhaled. "Tell you what. You fly back to Atlanta and I'll have one of my people drop the money off. Okay, my friend?"

"A'ight, ock."

"Okay, buddy. I have to go back in store. I call you," Wally assured as he got out of the Camaro and headed back in his store.

Khafre pulled out of the Brown Store and made a left on 25th Street when his phone rang. "Talk to me!" answered Khafre.

"Hey baby! I miss you so much," expressed Quen.

"I miss you too, ma. You a'ight?"

"Yeah, I am. Um, when will you be back?"

"Be there tonight, bae. Why?"

"I need to tell you something," Quen replied nervously.

"Okay, wassup?"

Quen drew in a deep breath and exhaled. "I'm pregnant."

"What?"

"We are having a baby."

"You sho'?"

"I took the test twice, baby. Are you mad? How do you feel about it?"

"I love that shit, girl."

Quen laughed. "He says he loves it, Mama."

"Who you talking to?"

"My mother-in-law. Who else?"

"Tell my mama I love her and I'll see y'all tonight."

"Okay, baby, I love you."

"I love you, too."

Khafre hung up the phone as a warm feeling fanned all through his body. After losing his father, he vowed that if he ever had a child, he would be there relentlessly for him or her.

"I'm 'bout to be a father, Pops!" Khafre yelled out loud as if his father was in the car with him.

Khafre made a left and pulled into the medical center. Before going inside, he tried calling Cowboy's number once more. This time the phone was answered.

"Damn, nigga! I been trying to call you past foreva, nigga!" Khafre stated.

"Khafre! It's been a while, Cuz!"

Khafre could recognize Hezron's voice from anywhere. He also knew that Cowboy had to dead if Hezron had his phone.

"How you been, family? How ya shoulder holding up?" clowned Khafre.

"Oh, it's in tip top shape! Too bad I can't say the same for you, homie." Hezron laughed demonically.

"Too bad we can't say the same for ya pops! How 'bout ya moms? Huh? Can't forget about Amber, can we? That bitch had you pussy whipped! A bitch flick ya li'l balls the right way and you cuff her. I know you fucked up behind that one, but that's the price we pay for attachments," schooled Khafre, remembering the words of his father. "You know I'on kill kids, but it is what it wrote," Khafre pronounced icily.

Hezron sat and took in all that Khafre had laid on him. Dough-boy could see murder in his eyes as he gripped the phone tightly.

"You a'ight, homie?" Doughboy asked, concerned.

Hezron ignored him.

"And what about'cha, brother? I hear he can't even hold a conversation yet."

"Don't trip. I'ma kill you and ya momma!"

"Good luck wit' that one. I'm finna go in here and check on my cousin. You know see if I can get 'em to talk to me. Oh yeah! That nigga you prolly done put in Taylor's Creek, ain't my homie. I just met 'em, stupid!" Click!

***

Khafre stepped out of his whip with the red flag that the voodoo priest gave him in his right back pocket when his phone rang. "Yeah!"

"Hey daddy."

"Who the fuck is this?"

"It's Hanna and Samantha," replied Hanna.

"How the hell you get my number?"

"Your mother gave it to me." Khafre made a mental note to check his mother about giving his number out. "Is that a problem?"

"Not at all. It's nice to hear from y'all, but I'm in the middle of something right now. You can call me back?"

"This won't take long," Hanna assured.

"Okay, wassup?"

"Did you hear what happened to Jarrod?"

"Nall, what happened?"

"They found his yacht abandoned and bloody, but haven't found him yet."

"Damn, that's some wild shit."

"I know."

"That's why you called me?"

"That's one of the reasons, yes."

"What else?"

"You have two kids that you don't know about."

"Da fuck? By who?"

"Me and Samantha. You have two little boys that were born a day apart. Their names are Hassan and Husain, three years old."

Khafre took a minute to process what he'd just heard as the elevator door closed. "So why y'all ain't been tell me this shit!"

"Really, daddy? You changed your number."

"Damn, that's right. My fault. I had a lot going on."

"We know."

"Where's Samantha?"

"In another room with Husain."

"Where y'all at? I wanna see my sons."

"In Naples, daddy."

"A'ight, I'ma call y'all back tonight. Make sho y'all pick up."

"Okay, we love you!"

"Yeah, yeah!"

Khafre hung the phone up and exited the elevator. He was elated to find out that he had two sons. He just didn't know how he was gon' tell Quen, and that they were from two twin white girls. Khafre pushed it all to the back of his mind as he entered room 305. He noticed Crystal sitting by Machi's bedside on the left. When he fixed his eyes on Machi, he saw that Machi's eyes were open.

"Hey Khafre," greeted Crystal, unaware of the beef that was up there stuck there.

Khafre ignored her. Unable to talk due to the bullet that had entered his neck, a wave of panic enveloped Machi's body causing the cardiogram to beep rapidly.

"Oh my God, Machi, baby, what's wrong?" She looked at Khafre, who was smiling horridly, then back at Machi, whose eyes were now twice their size.

"Baby, it's just your cousin, what's wrong?" When Crystal glanced back at Khafre, he was pointing a FN-509 with a suppressor directly at Machi. "What dey do, nigga?"

To Be Continued…
Killa Kounty 4
Coming Soon

Lock Down Publications and Ca$h Presents assisted publishing packages.

BASIC PACKAGE $499
Editing
Cover Design
Formatting

UPGRADED PACKAGE $800
Typing
Editing
Cover Design
Formatting

ADVANCE PACKAGE $1,200
Typing
Editing
Cover Design
Formatting
Copyright registration
Proofreading
Upload book to Amazon

LDP SUPREME PACKAGE $1,500
Typing
Editing
Cover Design
Formatting
Copyright registration
Proofreading
Set up Amazon account
Upload book to Amazon
Advertise on LDP Amazon and Facebook page

***Other services available upon request. Additional charges
may apply
Lock Down Publications
P.O. Box 944
Stockbridge, GA 30281-9998
Phone # 470 303-9761

Khufu

Submission Guideline

Submit the first three chapters of your completed manuscript to ldpsubmissions@gmail.com, subject line: Your book's title. The manuscript must be in a .doc file and sent as an attachment. Document should be in Times New Roman, double spaced and in size 12 font. Also, provide your synopsis and full contact information. If sending multiple submissions, they must each be in a separate email.

Have a story but no way to send it electronically? You can still submit to LDP/Ca$h Presents. Send in the first three chapters, written or typed, of your completed manuscript to:

LDP: Submissions Dept
Po Box 944
Stockbridge, Ga 30281

DO NOT send original manuscript. Must be a duplicate.

Provide your synopsis and a cover letter containing your full contact information.

Thanks for considering LDP and Ca$h Presents.

NEW RELEASES

BABY, I'M WINTERTIME COLD by MEESHA

ANGEL 4 by ANTHONY FIELDS

HOOD CONSIGLIERE 2 by KEESE

KILLA KOUNTY by KHUFU

Coming Soon from Lock Down Publications/Ca$h Presents

BLOOD OF A BOSS **VI**

SHADOWS OF THE GAME II

TRAP BASTARD II

By **Askari**

LOYAL TO THE GAME **IV**

By **T.J. & Jelissa**

TRUE SAVAGE **VIII**

MIDNIGHT CARTEL IV

DOPE BOY MAGIC IV

CITY OF KINGZ III

NIGHTMARE ON SILENT AVE II

THE PLUG OF LIL MEXICO II

CLASSIC CITY II

By **Chris Green**

BLAST FOR ME **III**

A SAVAGE DOPEBOY III

CUTTHROAT MAFIA III

DUFFLE BAG CARTEL VII

HEARTLESS GOON VI

By **Ghost**

A HUSTLER'S DECEIT III

KILL ZONE II

BAE BELONGS TO ME III

TIL DEATH II

By **Aryanna**

KING OF THE TRAP III

By **T.J. Edwards**

GORILLAZ IN THE BAY V

3X KRAZY III

STRAIGHT BEAST MODE III

De'Kari

KINGPIN KILLAZ IV

STREET KINGS III

PAID IN BLOOD III

CARTEL KILLAZ IV

DOPE GODS III

Hood Rich

SINS OF A HUSTLA II

ASAD

RICH $AVAGE III

By Martell Troublesome Bolden

YAYO V

Bred In The Game 2

S. Allen

THE STREETS WILL TALK II

By Yolanda Moore

SON OF A DOPE FIEND III

HEAVEN GOT A GHETTO II

SKI MASK MONEY II

By Renta

LOYALTY AIN'T PROMISED III

By Keith Williams

I'M NOTHING WITHOUT HIS LOVE II

SINS OF A THUG II

TO THE THUG I LOVED BEFORE II

IN A HUSTLER I TRUST II

By Monet Dragun

QUIET MONEY IV

EXTENDED CLIP III

Khufu

THUG LIFE IV

By **Trai'Quan**

THE STREETS MADE ME IV

By **Larry D. Wright**

IF YOU CROSS ME ONCE II

ANGEL V

By **Anthony Fields**

THE STREETS WILL NEVER CLOSE IV

By **K'ajji**

HARD AND RUTHLESS III

KILLA KOUNTY IV

By **Khufu**

MONEY GAME III

By **Smoove Dolla**

JACK BOYS VS DOPE BOYS IV

A GANGSTA'S QUR'AN V

COKE GIRLZ II

COKE BOYS II

LIFE OF A SAVAGE V

CHI'RAQ GANGSTAS V

By **Romell Tukes**

MURDA WAS THE CASE III

Elijah R. Freeman

THE STREETS NEVER LET GO III

By **Robert Baptiste**

AN UNFORESEEN LOVE IV

BABY, I'M WINTERTIME COLD II

By **Meesha**

MONEY MAFIA II

By **Jibril Williams**

QUEEN OF THE ZOO III

By **Black Migo**

VICIOUS LOYALTY III

By **Kingpen**

A GANGSTA'S PAIN III

By **J-Blunt**

CONFESSIONS OF A JACKBOY III

By **Nicholas Lock**

GRIMEY WAYS III

By **Ray Vinci**

KING KILLA II

By **Vincent "Vitto" Holloway**

BETRAYAL OF A THUG II

By **Fre$h**

THE MURDER QUEENS III

By **Michael Gallon**

THE BIRTH OF A GANGSTER III

By **Delmont Player**

TREAL LOVE II

By **Le'Monica Jackson**

FOR THE LOVE OF BLOOD II

By **Jamel Mitchell**

RAN OFF ON DA PLUG II

By **Paper Boi Rari**

HOOD CONSIGLIERE III

By **Keese**

PRETTY GIRLS DO NASTY THINGS II

By **Nicole Goosby**

PROTÉGÉ OF A LEGEND II

Khufu

By Corey Robinson
IT'S JUST ME AND YOU II
By Ah'Million
BORN IN THE GRAVE II
By Self Made Tay
FOREVER GANGSTA III
By Adrian Dulan
GORILLAZ IN THE TRENCHES II
By SayNoMore

Available Now

RESTRAINING ORDER **I & II**
By **CA$H & Coffee**
LOVE KNOWS NO BOUNDARIES **I II & III**
By **Coffee**
RAISED AS A GOON I, II, III & IV
BRED BY THE SLUMS I, II, III
BLAST FOR ME I & II
ROTTEN TO THE CORE I II III
A BRONX TALE I, II, III
DUFFLE BAG CARTEL I II III IV V VI
HEARTLESS GOON I II III IV V
A SAVAGE DOPEBOY I II

DRUG LORDS I II III

CUTTHROAT MAFIA I II

KING OF THE TRENCHES

By **Ghost**

LAY IT DOWN **I & II**

LAST OF A DYING BREED I II

BLOOD STAINS OF A SHOTTA I & II III

By **Jamaica**

LOYAL TO THE GAME I II III

LIFE OF SIN I, II III

By **TJ & Jelissa**

BLOODY COMMAS I & II

SKI MASK CARTEL I II & III

KING OF NEW YORK I II,III IV V

RISE TO POWER I II III

COKE KINGS I II III IV V

BORN HEARTLESS I II III IV

KING OF THE TRAP I II

By **T.J. Edwards**

IF LOVING HIM IS WRONG…I & II

LOVE ME EVEN WHEN IT HURTS I II III

By **Jelissa**

WHEN THE STREETS CLAP BACK I & II III

THE HEART OF A SAVAGE I II III IV

MONEY MAFIA

LOYAL TO THE SOIL I II III

By **Jibril Williams**

A DISTINGUISHED THUG STOLE MY HEART I II & III

LOVE SHOULDN'T HURT I II III IV

RENEGADE BOYS I II III IV

Khufu

PAID IN KARMA I II III
SAVAGE STORMS I II III
AN UNFORESEEN LOVE I II III
BABY, I'M WINTERTIME COLD
By **Meesha**
A GANGSTER'S CODE I &, II III
A GANGSTER'S SYN I II III
THE SAVAGE LIFE I II III
CHAINED TO THE STREETS I II III
BLOOD ON THE MONEY I II III
A GANGSTA'S PAIN I II
By J-Blunt
PUSH IT TO THE LIMIT
By **Bre' Hayes**
BLOOD OF A BOSS **I, II, III, IV, V**
SHADOWS OF THE GAME
TRAP BASTARD
By **Askari**
THE STREETS BLEED MURDER **I, II & III**
THE HEART OF A GANGSTA I II& III
By **Jerry Jackson**
CUM FOR ME I II III IV V VI VII VIII
An **LDP Erotica Collaboration**
BRIDE OF A HUSTLA **I II & II**
THE FETTI GIRLS **I, II& III**
CORRUPTED BY A GANGSTA I, II III, IV
BLINDED BY HIS LOVE
THE PRICE YOU PAY FOR LOVE I, II ,III
DOPE GIRL MAGIC I II III
By **Destiny Skai**

WHEN A GOOD GIRL GOES BAD
By **Adrienne**
THE COST OF LOYALTY I II III
By Kweli
A GANGSTER'S REVENGE **I II III & IV**
THE BOSS MAN'S DAUGHTERS I II III IV V
A SAVAGE LOVE **I & II**
BAE BELONGS TO ME I II
A HUSTLER'S DECEIT I, II, III
WHAT BAD BITCHES DO I, II, III
SOUL OF A MONSTER I II III
KILL ZONE
A DOPE BOY'S QUEEN I II III
TIL DEATH
By **Aryanna**
A KINGPIN'S AMBITON
A KINGPIN'S AMBITION **II**
I MURDER FOR THE DOUGH
By **Ambitious**
TRUE SAVAGE I II III IV V VI VII
DOPE BOY MAGIC I, II, III
MIDNIGHT CARTEL I II III
CITY OF KINGZ I II
NIGHTMARE ON SILENT AVE
THE PLUG OF LIL MEXICO II
CLASSIC CITY
By **Chris Green**
A DOPEBOY'S PRAYER
By **Eddie "Wolf" Lee**
THE KING CARTEL **I, II & III**

Khufu

By **Frank Gresham**
THESE NIGGAS AIN'T LOYAL **I, II & III**
By **Nikki Tee**
GANGSTA SHYT **I II &III**
By **CATO**
THE ULTIMATE BETRAYAL
By **Phoenix**
BOSS'N UP **I , II & III**
By **Royal Nicole**
I LOVE YOU TO DEATH
By **Destiny J**
I RIDE FOR MY HITTA
I STILL RIDE FOR MY HITTA
By **Misty Holt**
LOVE & CHASIN' PAPER
By **Qay Crockett**
TO DIE IN VAIN
SINS OF A HUSTLA
By **ASAD**
BROOKLYN HUSTLAZ
By **Boogsy Morina**
BROOKLYN ON LOCK I & II
By **Sonovia**
GANGSTA CITY
By **Teddy Duke**
A DRUG KING AND HIS DIAMOND I & II III
A DOPEMAN'S RICHES
HER MAN, MINE'S TOO I, II
CASH MONEY HO'S
THE WIFEY I USED TO BE I II

PRETTY GIRLS DO NASTY THINGS

By Nicole Goosby

TRAPHOUSE KING **I II & III**

KINGPIN KILLAZ I II III

STREET KINGS I II

PAID IN BLOOD **I II**

CARTEL KILLAZ I II III

DOPE GODS I II

By **Hood Rich**

LIPSTICK KILLAH **I, II, III**

CRIME OF PASSION I II & III

FRIEND OR FOE I II III

By **Mimi**

STEADY MOBBN' **I, II, III**

THE STREETS STAINED MY SOUL I II III

By **Marcellus Allen**

WHO SHOT YA **I, II, III**

SON OF A DOPE FIEND I II

HEAVEN GOT A GHETTO

SKI MASK MONEY

Renta

GORILLAZ IN THE BAY **I II III IV**

TEARS OF A GANGSTA I II

3X KRAZY I II

STRAIGHT BEAST MODE I II

DE'KARI

TRIGGADALE I II III

MURDAROBER WAS THE CASE I II

Elijah R. Freeman

GOD BLESS THE TRAPPERS I, II, III

Khufu

THESE SCANDALOUS STREETS I, II, III

FEAR MY GANGSTA I, II, III IV, V

THESE STREETS DON'T LOVE NOBODY I, II

BURY ME A G I, II, III, IV, V

A GANGSTA'S EMPIRE I, II, III, IV

THE DOPEMAN'S BODYGAURD I II

THE REALEST KILLAZ I II III

THE LAST OF THE OGS I II III

Tranay Adams

THE STREETS ARE CALLING

Duquie Wilson

MARRIED TO A BOSS I II III

By Destiny Skai & Chris Green

KINGZ OF THE GAME I II III IV V VI

Playa Ray

SLAUGHTER GANG I II III

RUTHLESS HEART I II III

By Willie Slaughter

FUK SHYT

By Blakk Diamond

DON'T F#CK WITH MY HEART I II

By Linnea

ADDICTED TO THE DRAMA I II III

IN THE ARM OF HIS BOSS II

By Jamila

YAYO I II III IV

A SHOOTER'S AMBITION I II

BRED IN THE GAME

By S. Allen

TRAP GOD I II III

RICH $AVAGE I II
MONEY IN THE GRAVE I II III
By Martell Troublesome Bolden
FOREVER GANGSTA I II
GLOCKS ON SATIN SHEETS I II
By Adrian Dulan
TOE TAGZ I II III IV
LEVELS TO THIS SHYT I II
IT'S JUST ME AND YOU
By Ah'Million
KINGPIN DREAMS I II III
RAN OFF ON DA PLUG
By Paper Boi Rari
CONFESSIONS OF A GANGSTA I II III IV
CONFESSIONS OF A JACKBOY I II
By Nicholas Lock
I'M NOTHING WITHOUT HIS LOVE
SINS OF A THUG
TO THE THUG I LOVED BEFORE
A GANGSTA SAVED XMAS
IN A HUSTLER I TRUST
By Monet Dragun
CAUGHT UP IN THE LIFE I II III
THE STREETS NEVER LET GO I II
By Robert Baptiste
NEW TO THE GAME I II III
MONEY, MURDER & MEMORIES I II III
By **Malik D. Rice**
LIFE OF A SAVAGE I II III IV
A GANGSTA'S QUR'AN I II III IV

Khufu

MURDA SEASON I II III

GANGLAND CARTEL I II III

CHI'RAQ GANGSTAS I II III IV

KILLERS ON ELM STREET I II III

JACK BOYZ N DA BRONX I II III

A DOPEBOY'S DREAM I II III

JACK BOYS VS DOPE BOYS I II III

COKE GIRLZ

COKE BOYS

By Romell Tukes

LOYALTY AIN'T PROMISED I II

By Keith Williams

QUIET MONEY I II III

THUG LIFE I II III

EXTENDED CLIP I II

A GANGSTA'S PARADISE

By **Trai'Quan**

THE STREETS MADE ME I II III

By **Larry D. Wright**

THE ULTIMATE SACRIFICE I, II, III, IV, V, VI

KHADIFI

IF YOU CROSS ME ONCE

ANGEL I II III IV

IN THE BLINK OF AN EYE

By **Anthony Fields**

THE LIFE OF A HOOD STAR

By Ca$h & Rashia Wilson

THE STREETS WILL NEVER CLOSE I II III

By K'ajji

CREAM I II III

206

THE STREETS WILL TALK
By Yolanda Moore
NIGHTMARES OF A HUSTLA I II III
By King Dream
CONCRETE KILLA I II III
VICIOUS LOYALTY I II
By Kingpen
HARD AND RUTHLESS I II
MOB TOWN 251
THE BILLIONAIRE BENTLEYS I II III
By Von Diesel
GHOST MOB
Stilloan Robinson
MOB TIES I II III IV V VI
SOUL OF A HUSTLER, HEART OF A KILLER
GORILLAZ IN THE TRENCHES
By SayNoMore
BODYMORE MURDERLAND I II III
THE BIRTH OF A GANGSTER I II
By Delmont Player
FOR THE LOVE OF A BOSS
By C. D. Blue
MOBBED UP I II III IV
THE BRICK MAN I II III IV
THE COCAINE PRINCESS I II III IV V
By King Rio
KILLA KOUNTY I II III IV
By Khufu
MONEY GAME I II
By Smoove Dolla

Khufu

A GANGSTA'S KARMA I II
By FLAME
KING OF THE TRENCHES I II III
by **GHOST & TRANAY ADAMS**
QUEEN OF THE ZOO I II
By **Black Migo**
GRIMEY WAYS I II
By Ray Vinci
XMAS WITH AN ATL SHOOTER
By Ca$h & Destiny Skai
KING KILLA
By Vincent "Vitto" Holloway
BETRAYAL OF A THUG
By Fre$h
THE MURDER QUEENS I II
By Michael Gallon
TREAL LOVE
By Le'Monica Jackson
FOR THE LOVE OF BLOOD
By Jamel Mitchell
HOOD CONSIGLIERE I II
By Keese
PROTÉGÉ OF A LEGEND
By Corey Robinson
BORN IN THE GRAVE
By Self Made Tay
MOAN IN MY MOUTH
By XTASY
TORN BETWEEN A GANGSTER AND A GENTLEMAN
By J-BLUNT & Miss Kim

BOOKS BY LDP'S CEO, CA$H

TRUST IN NO MAN

TRUST IN NO MAN 2

TRUST IN NO MAN 3

BONDED BY BLOOD

SHORTY GOT A THUG

THUGS CRY

THUGS CRY 2

THUGS CRY 3

TRUST NO BITCH

TRUST NO BITCH 2

TRUST NO BITCH 3

TIL MY CASKET DROPS

RESTRAINING ORDER

RESTRAINING ORDER 2

IN LOVE WITH A CONVICT

LIFE OF A HOOD STAR

XMAS WITH AN ATL SHOOTER

Khufu

CPSIA information can be obtained
at www.ICGtesting.com
Printed in the USA
BVHW051641140523
664015BV00019B/192

9 781958 111581